Sunce tatino, nadam se da nećeš zaboraviti bosanski jezik i da ćeš jednog dana moći čitati tatine knjige.

Do tada, puno te volim i jedva čekam da te vidim.

Tvoj tata,

Dario Džamonja.

Sar. 12. jul, 2001.

Dad's Sun,

I hope you don't forget the Bosnian language, and that one day you'll be able to read dad's books. Until then, I love you a lot and I can't wait to see you.

Your dad,
Džario Damonja
Sar. 12. Jul. 2001

Letters from the Madhouse

Dario Džamonja

Translated by
Nevena Džamonja

Mercurial Editions
MMXXV

Introduction

Nevena Džamonja

I am not a translator by profession. I have no formal education in Bosnian and did not attend school there, so learning how to read and write as a teenager left me feeling developmentally stunted, ashamed of my missteps, and has been a labor which I took upon myself to stay connected to my birthplace and a family that has been left fragmented by time and geography. This work itself is not an ordinary work of literary translation, as there is no distance between myself and the writer, my father. As well, I am not interested in the translation of words, but rather transferences of meaning, mapping a history through a written and emotional archive. My father was not present for much of my life, and reading his work has been an attempted means of trying to find clarity or answers to questions that I have not been able to answer. Namely those of family and personal history, an explanation of what happened, and why, that has led my life to where it is now? If nostalgia is a privilege or if memory is a prison?

The book speaks for itself. The narrator is often dislikable, gruff, pitiful, comical, tender, but always insightful and self-aware. Alcohol is the most pervasive theme, along with alienation, both internal and external. Dario's mentality often feels archaic, embodying a type of street roughness and machismo that is performative, but prevalent and inevitably shaped his trajectory. As was obvious to those around him then, and to himself, this was a product of trauma and that alienation. To remedy it, he built a wall against the outside world, he balanced tragedy and humor in every story, approaching them in a heartbreakingly truthful and ego-less manner. He romanticized isolation and exile, and a refusal of basic needs even before the war. This was the shell of someone who felt abandoned and exiled throughout his life, and only saw the cafes and bars of Sarajevo as his home. Someone who didn't believe much in himself except for in his ability to write.

This book is also a personal account of displacement, and of war and its mental and physical wounds. It is his only book written in America, but like all his books, is about Sarajevo. The chronology isn't linear, but tells the story of the final toll that America took on his life. Ultimately, he died of liver cirrhosis in 2001. At that point he had returned to Bosnia and had been living there for a few years, hoping to regain some semblance of normalcy. He wrote that he would rather die a writer in Sarajevo than a dishwasher in America, and that he did. While not explicitly about the fall of Yugoslavia, that context cannot be ignored when reading this book. Apart from the bloody and violent dissolution of civic society, a greater ideal was lost. One that differed greatly from the American Dream, in that it offered the promise of some semblance of equality and security through education, health care, housing, and ideologies of brotherhood and unity. Things that have no place in American society.

To call the writing colloquial would be an understatement. His writing is a primer on Sarajevan slang, some of which is incomprehensible to even other Yugoslavs and often untranslatable outside of a Sarajevan context. The book is a testament to the oral history of Sarajevo; it is a cheeky inside joke that name drops people and places of a bygone area and is immediately recognizable to those from the city. I have included endnotes for terms or places that feel relevant for comprehension, but some I have left unexplained because Sarajevo isn't meant for every outsider to understand. It stretches in endless sentences, a stream of consciousness that is punctuated with parenthetical tangents rather than sentence endings; a language of rolling neurosis and rumination. While they're technically non-fiction, Dario's stories always contained elements of what could generously be described as magical realism, and realistically described as dramatized exaggeration. He ascribes complex quotes and knowledge of Bosnian rock to an American one-and-a-half-year-old daughter, claims he was just barely missed by a tornado that leveled a nearby town (this tornado actually hit in 1984), characters and references show up in the form of secret nods (a mention of a mild but evil stepmother, a Hungarian porter with the same name as his stepfather), among many other half-truths. To American readers, comments on ethnicity and sexuality will seem dated, but Westerners often forget that the diversity of their countries is a legacy of slavery and post-colonial migration - something that Yugoslavia didn't have.

Putting aside my own resentments with an absent father, I have found more space for compassion in the years since he died and since I have grown older. His own relationship with himself was complicated as he was a person shrouded in the mythos of his own trauma. His parents divorced early in his life, first with his mother remarrying and eventually moving to Amsterdam. He was cared for by his uncle Neven, my namesake, who he greatly looked up to as he was handsome, charming, well-liked and well-known in Sarajevo. Neven committed suicide at the age of twenty-seven, initiating a repetitive cycle of abandonment that came to cloud Dario's existence. His father eventually remarried as well, and when he did, his new wife decided that Dario could not live with them, so he was sent to live with his grandparents. While he adored and respected them, he grew up in poverty and in the freedom of neglect that flavored his temperament and became his gateway into alcohol and the underground of Sarajevo. My grandfather's second marriage eventually dissolved, and after that he bought an apartment and invited my father to join him again. My father refused, and my grandfather hung himself shortly thereafter in that apartment, which my father inherited, and in which I was born. When my mother moved in after their marriage, she found a stained old tuxedo tucked in a closet and asked my father what it was. It was the suit my grandfather was wearing when he killed himself, and she made him throw it out.

By the time I was born, my father was already a celebrated writer. Since high school, he had been ingratiated into the world of the Sarajevo underground, hanging around with petty criminals, poets, and other bohemian characters in cafes that seemed to endlessly pop up along the strip of valley that Sarajevo occupies. There he found a family for himself, and a life's purpose writing weekly columns, prose and short stories about the city he loved. His drinking was legendary and well-documented by family and friends. It was also the root from which all his sabotage stemmed. When the war started, he vehemently spoke out against the waves of nationalism that began to ripple throughout Yugoslavia and tear it to shreds. My mother and I left Sarajevo for a refugee camp in an early convoy for women and children, meanwhile my father was injured by a grenade and stayed in Sarajevo with my maternal grandmother. When we eventually went to America as refugees, my father and grandmother, as well as some other family, joined us later on.

In America he found no way to assimilate, nor did he want to. His alcoholism and womanizing became worse. Many things about America were incomprehensible to him, mostly American people, whom he generally saw as cultureless and unsympathetic. The alienation he faced in America was the final straw that destroyed him. He was incapable of existing outside of Sarajevo. He was not the first, and not the last, to face such degradation in

America. As we see now more than ever, America is a machine that is built on alienation and abuse, it glorifies violence and inhumanity, offering no comfort for those who have crossed its borders. America, which sets its sights on the destruction of Palestine and treats those at its borders with utmost contempt; tells us to shovel shit, to be happy with "opportunities", to shut up because our misery and poverty are too upsetting and disruptive to the placated American mind; one too dull to recognize the limits of its own raptures, too privileged to desire solidarity.

As time passes, I have come to learn that life is merely a collection of stories, people, experiences, and places. The information people choose to disclose or withhold, to themselves or to others, is a reflection of their subjective truth; their own fears, their own delusions, or the trappings of their own (dis)comfort. I know that there is a divide between the physicality of existence and the elusive salvation of mental peace. We sustain, create, and even erase memories as a means of narrative. I've been trying to learn that what is done is done, what has passed is passed, what happened happened, but I think for some people it is better to live in their memories. Maybe not exactly as they were, but distilled down through the lens of hindsight, to what mattered most or what was most beautiful, or maybe what sounded best. Some people possess a type of nostalgia, sadness, and an overwhelming sense of sentimentality embedded in them. That sentimentality, when paired with active disassociation, under the imposed conditions of degradation, can become a rot that spreads up from the root, leaving the flesh a heap of damp sluggish remorse, something that ultimately destroys them in a world parallel to that of their memories.

No great closure came from translating this book. I am even left with new questions, and maybe some new insights. Most importantly, though, I know that Dario was a person who I could relate to quite well. At times I felt extreme sadness for the orphaned schoolboy, who at the first blossom of Spring, would pick wildflower bouquets from every corner of Sarajevo for his grandmother, whom he loved dearly. At others, I felt disgust for the grizzled alcoholic with an abrasive sense of humor, who would seemingly derail everything around him. Reading his stories, I'm always shocked to see how much I am his daughter. A wild boy with a rocker streak and a hatred of authority and the pretension of the bourgeoisie; a man with an affinity and solidarity for the outcasts and misfits, who carried a vast emptiness that was only satiated by untempered self-destruction - characteristics I know all too well. I have seen myself mirrored in my father's stories since the first time I read one. That mirroring is one of unsettled anxiety and sadness that has felt like it was imprinted into my bones. The loneliness that comes up throughout the book is one that I know well. It's an undercurrent of sadness that is so overwhelming and inexplicable that at times I feel that I am feeling a dozen other people's sadness concentrated in myself. I too have punctured my own narrative with annihilation. I am not someone who has ever felt welcomed into the bosom of life. I often am more dispositioned to dwell in the comfort of my own misery, alone on my own terms, than to try and find solace under Sisyphean conditions. I have spent decades absorbing a hatred and bitterness in myself, an (un)natural hardening that was a reaction to abandonment but ultimately a wall built to avoid acknowledging my own sadness of something that I lost, that I too was displaced from. That thing, as I've come to understand it, is a sense of belonging, a sense of home; the lack from which that cosmic loneliness stems. In this sense, I am thankful for my own connections to my own undergrounds and to my own outcasts who have provided me with a sense of kinship in ways similar to what Dario had in his Sarajevo. For many years I tried to avoid the precarity of nostalgia, choosing nihilism over sentimentality. However, I have grown softer as I have gotten older, or maybe this is just something I inherited after all. Now it leads me to fear what dead people think of me, and cling to the bittersweetness of my own memories and others'.

Thank you to Lana for her help with editing the text; to Cay, Sophie, Christian, and Zanie for providing a tranquil escape where I could work and work out my demons in peace, to Everett for the heavy lifting in times when I could barely lift myself up; my Mother Dijana, Aunts Buca and Vesna for the context; Sanja for her expertise with words; countless other friends in New York, Berlin, Sarajevo, and beyond for enduring my chaos. I believe in ghosts, and I think a few were around for this: Borka, Dario and Quincy.

Letters from the Madhouse

To Nevena and Vesna,
Daughters without a Father,

Dad

A Bridge Called Desire

While I write this, in front of my eyes appears a caricature that I saw a long time ago in a newspaper: two guys stand on opposite sides of the street, in between them is an endless stream of traffic, they yell between themselves:

"Friend, how did you cross the street?"
"I didn't. I was born on this side."

This caricature is a sad reality in Sarajevo, where the Vrbanja Bridge has divided the city and has become a living illustration, for both monsters and normal people, of the unthinkable project to separate Bosnia and Herzegovina along "ethnic borders" and "ethnically clean entities." People who had friends in Grbavica, a neighborhood on the left bank of the river, which at the beginning of the war found itself in the hands of the *Chetniks*, can with an easy soul forget about them; people who had friends in America or Australia or Grbavica could expect to see those in America and Australia before those in Grbavica; people who one day (as every previous day) went to work on the right side of the river or who that day hung around a bit longer with their friends in a cafe, were stuck where they were - separated from their families, without their hard earned money in their pocket, in the same pair of pants and shirts, refugees in the city they were born in.

It's not like we didn't have a sense of life on the "other side." The SRNA - the nationalist Serbian television channel from Pale - would every day broadcast episodes about the "idyllic life" in Serbian Sarajevo.

While thousands and thousands of Sarajevans, in between breaks of heavy artillery and running through "sniper alley," searched parks for anything they could find that could function as food; birch bark, nettle, dandelion, linden flowers, or snails, the SRNA would broadcast the full markets in Grbavica (which wasn't even a lie because 90% of the aid that was meant for Sarajevans ended up in the hands of the Chetniks), and "warm" welcomes to the "liberators" from Montenegro and Serbia wearing *šubare* with cockades of the Serbian flag, daggers on their belts, who, who knows why I guess, came to defend what was "theirs." (How much Sarajevo was "theirs" is best attested to by the fact that a dozen of them were captured when they had drunkenly wandered through an unknown city and ended up across our lines.)

The first exchange of citizens began in the middle of the summer. I emphasize citizens, because this wasn't a matter of prisoners of war, but rather ordinary people. Those who found themselves (or were born) on "the wrong side." Everyone who crossed the Vrbanja, the "bridge called desire," were welcomed as if they had risen from the dead, and they impatiently pressed about the fate of others, their family or friends.

That's how it was when one morning Mahir showed up at the benches of the Soccer Club Sarajevo. Although a severe scarcity ruled, and every German mark (which by then was the only means of payment) would be carefully calculated before being spent, Mahir's table was packed with drinks.

Mahir was laughing, "Slow down, people. Drinks for everyone on my tab!"

That's what was extremely strange, because we knew "the lucky ones" who were able to cross weren't allowed to bring anything of value - even women of all ages were given "gynecological exams."

And then Mahir began his story...

He lived across the street from the butcher Majmunović in Grbavica. (Majmunović was the most well-known and richest butcher in the city, a Serb.)

For Muslims like Mahir, it was prohibited to walk the streets freely and they weren't on the food distribution list, but Majmunović, now in his camouflage uniform in place of a butcher's apron, and with a Kalashnikov in hand, nearly every morning would kick Mahir's door and threaten him saying, "Open up, *balija*, or I'll break the door down!"

Mahir would open the door, and Majmunović would enter, cursing at the top of his voice. Then Majmunović would take some food, sometimes a bottle of *rakija*, cigarettes, and coffee from his backpack... They'd sit and talk about the insanity around them, they'd drink and smoke, as was the norm, and occasionally Majmunović would scream "Give me your money or I'll slaughter you right here. Fuck your Mother, you *balija*, I know you hid it somewhere and I won't stop until I find it!" just loud enough that the neighbors, Chetnik informants, could hear how zealously he took pride in his mistreatment and humiliation of Muslims.

That was all until one day the butcher showed up as usual, knocked on the door, but this time with a gigantic young man in a uniform.

Mahir, who was a basketball referee, recognized the kid as a local player from the team Ilidža, and the kid recognized him.

"Ref, give me the money, the gold, all of it - you better not try to slip some for yourself!"

He was dead serious and Mahir took out his savings (a few thousand German marks, his wife's jewelry, and he even took his wedding band off his finger). The kid stopped to think about the wedding band but, even so, he stuffed it into a plastic bag and emphatically said, "We'll see each other again, Ref..." which didn't sound encouraging in the least.

Not too long after that, on the Bridge of Brotherhood and Unity (the irony!), Mahir found himself in a group of people meant to be exchanged, which happened to be led by that same kid.

When it was Mahir's turn in line, the kid came up to him and handed him the plastic bag:

"It's all there, you don't have to count it, Ref. May God help you."

Mahir's story deeply touched and cheered us up, because he gave us hope that with all of what was happening, man could rise above the animal in himself, and that life, despite everything, would go on.

Sadly, this isn't the only story Mahir told us...

We all knew and remembered Iris. She was one of the most beautiful girls in high school. She finished her gastroenterology degree and worked at the hospital for a bit, then she got married, and, because her husband was from one of the most well-known and richest Sarajevan families, she opened a private dental clinic, had wonderful children, and ended up with the misfortune of being a Serb married to a Muslim.

Within the first few days of the war, her husband (like many other respected and wealthy Muslims) was arrested for the "crime" of being Muslim, and was taken to a camp, and, just as misfortunes never come alone, circumstance confirmed that the "commander" of the quarter that Iris lived in was Božo Debelnogić, a creature who before the war had a lengthy police dossier, and, among all else, spent four years in the Zenica prison for rape. Mahir told us that Božo first tried "tenderness" with Iris: he promised he'd get her husband out of the camp and that he'd make sure her and the kids would be allowed to go wherever they wanted.

He was rejected with total disgust.

It didn't take long or much for his mood to change - a bottle of *rakija*.

He raped her first, and then he let the rest of his "soldiers" rape her. And with that, he ordered that they all leave one hundred marks next to the bed after the rape.

It wasn't enough for him that this was all going on in front of her terrified children, so he gathered all of her neighbors to watch too.

He howled: "Watch, you *balijas*! And don't you ever say that Serbian soldiers don't pay for what they take!"

The money, of course, he took in the end, and what happened with Iris and her kids… may God help them.

***

I know that there are people who suspect the credibility of the testimonies coming out of the wartime hell of Bosnia and Sarajevo, but I don't have much to say to those people, except I give them a test of conscience: if you believe the first story, why don't you believe the second one?

If they are ready to only believe one of the stories, then they have failed the test.

Endnotes

Chetniks - A colloquial term for nationalist Serbian army, originating in WWI.

šubare - A black wool Serbian folk-hat that became a nationalist symbol.

balija - Derogatory term for a Muslim.

rakija - Balkan fruit brandy.

Footnote

We sat in the garden of Soccer Club Sarajevo.[1] We sat there under a grenade-broken poplar, under a glass canopy stitched with plastic bags in the cold half-dark.

I was drinking some kind of poison made from grapevines, and he, a coffee. He, after all the bullshit that comes with the excessive consumption of alcohol, decided he'd "cool it" this year.

I had one hundred marks in my pocket and I felt like they would last forever. I even had a couple packs of cigarettes in my pocket too and a whole carton at home.

Just as God commands - the open pack was on the table (everyone knows that what's on the table is up for grabs) and he,

---

1. A "garden" is something that implies flowers, sun, grass, some birds and insects, an apple tree or a half-painted plum, a lilac bush[2], a path poured with gravel, checkered tablecloths and wooden chairs painted green, and of course, a grill, so let the uninitiated understand this expression only figuratively.

2. I just remembered a joke: a drunk enters a textile store and asks the sales woman for a shirt the color of lilac. She tells him, unfortunately, we don't have that color. He tells her, "Are you fucking around with me? The display is full of shirts!" "But, comrade[3], those are white shirts." "Dear, haven't you ever heard of a white lilac?"

just as God commands, asks me if he could light one up...

"Dara, don't fuck with me..."
"I just want one, with my coffee..."
"Go fuck yourself."

Dara always had sad eyes. Even in his wildest inebriations, from behind all the poison and harsh words, he hid the deep wound of an animal, characteristic only of lonely people; in his wittiest outbursts, when the cafe burst out in laughter, his eyes dimly shone with sadness under his thick brow.

Hunger had cut even him in half, his eyes were drawn in even further back, and I didn't even see them when he said:

"Well, when THIS[4] is done, I'm going to get shitfaced."

A horrible question stayed frozen on my lips:

"But what if it never ends?"

P.S. In America I got the news that Dara, very far from his birthplace of Marijin Dvor, died in Požarevac. Did he get shitfaced before he died - I don't know.

---

3. That joke stems from those times when everyone called each other "comrade" and "gentleman" was used only in a joking context: at the post office window, or the bank, at the hospital, waiting at the railroad track, in unimaginably long and slow lines, when someone's complaint: "Is anyone motherfucking working here?" would be followed by an inevitable "Oooh, the gentleman is in a hurry. He's the only one in a hurry!"

With one exception: for Tito always, even though quietly, but like we really personally knew him, we'd say "Now that's a real gentleman."

4. THIS was a common euphemism for everything that was happening in Sarajevo: horror, death, fear, hunger - in one word - WAR. As if we wanted to dull that horrible word and all of its consequences through pure avoidance.

All I know is that everyday I silently ask myself:
"But what if it never ends, Dara, my bud?"

P.P.S. Discerning readers will ask: why are there so many footnotes in such a short story?

Because this story is titled what it is!

A Perfect Day in America

I served dinner, I did the dishes, distributed "meds," I sit in my room and I try not to feel sorry for myself. My glance always strays to the picture of my kids that I keep next to my bed, and something inside of me wants to break, to scream; I would gladly break everything around me, set the house on fire and hop in a taxi at this hour and pop over to Rešo's at *Šadrvan* and cry my soul out until morning. And tomorrow? Tomorrow is a new day - a new fate!

But I'm here where I am; not in a taxi, not at Rešo's Šadrvan, I don't even myself know how much soul or how many more tears I have left, but tomorrow is again a new day - the same fate!

I stare blankly at the television and really pretend to be interested in if Clinton fucked someone or not, and in front of my eyes parade mirages of my former life; glimpses of broken New Year's decorations from a Christmas tree in the snow by the intersection by Alipašino Mosque, a green jersey with the number eleven on the back, that I wore in school when the *papci* from Breza destroyed us at Mejtaš 11-1, the giant diamond ring on the hand of the owner of *Egipat*, a bloody heel of bread in the teeth of a dog after the bombing of Miskina... The phone rings and I automatically recite:

"Hello, Hill Home Care. May I help you?"

"Is it you by chance?"

"Mirsad! It's you? Where are you calling from?"

"From Sarajevo, from *Korzo*, where else…"

"Give me the number so I can call you…"

"I'm fucking with you. I'm here in America, in Florida…"

"How did you find me?"

"Long story. Your ex wife gave me this number. Oh boy, did you find a place and time to get divorced."

"Long story, my Mirso. You know I was wounded, that my wife and kid were in Baško Polje during the war, that I had all my papers to leave, travel orders from Večernji Dani, a new passport, confirmations from Nakaš - but all worth jack shit. Some big shot guy from the government says to me: "We'd let you go, but we're worried that you'd stay and what you'd write in Croatia!" That's when I totally broke. Listen; what exactly would I write? Me, a respected citizen of Zagreb! I go to Ciglane, to the refugee office… They offer me cigarettes, food, but I'm just looking for a satellite phone so I can reach my wife and kid. I get through to them, I talk some nonsense with my daughter and I cry a year's worth of tears. The man asks me if I have a passport. I say I do, and he says to me: if you want to go to Split, then it's right now! There's no packing, no farewells, no telling anyone who you're going with… Alright, I say. He issues me some fake confirmation that I work for them, tells me to lose it when I get to Croatia, and that he'll wipe my name from the computer - that we never saw each other or spoke. That's how it happened.

"What can I say, there was a lot of the *raja* from Sarajevo down there. Some I knew from before, some I didn't. Of course, I got wasted the first night, and in the morning my wife says if you think you can carry on with your old ways then you should have never come! What do I know! Maybe she's right. I don't know, my Miso, I'm not smart. In America - even worse. Some

Yanks looked out for us when we got there; everything that they would have thrown in the trash they stuffed into our house; they invite us to dinner, they lead us around like animals, show us to their family, their friends... One hundred times over I tell the same story - I'm already disgusted with myself. My wife never gets tired of telling the same story, how she spent the entire winter in Baško Polje, can you imagine, without boots, and my friend, I want to cry while in front me appear Hamić, Kilo, Neka, Doko, Manda and everyone from the *raja*; dead and alive. Everything hurts, everything disgusts me, I'm scared of everything. At my own sister's house, my daughter Nevena makes a dash for the balcony. She doesn't see that the screen for mosquitoes is down, and she smacks into it at full force and I jump up from my chair to check if the screen is still intact!!!

"Then I sit in the bathroom and I cry: Lord, what has become of me? Fuck it, my Mirsad. Let me call you instead."

"Eh, no. Think of me calling you like me taking you out for a drink. Anyways today I had a perfect day. First: I went to the basement to wash my laundry in the machine and I found two dollars in it - they fell out of someone's pocket. Then at the post office I got my food stamps. I go to the store across the street and buy some bullshit for a dollar and ten cents so I can get ninety cents back in change. Then I pretend like I forgot something, and I buy ice cream for Zlaja, my son... I take the change again and go buy beers. I know what you mean when you say you're scared of everything. That's why I go to another store, because I figure they're watching my every step, that they'll arrest me if I cough too loud on the street. On the way back home, in a park, I find a barely open box of Winstons. Sure, they're a little damp from the dew, but they're smokable. My lady and Zlaja went to visit some Americans and they won't be back until morning: I have cigarettes and I have beers...

"I don't know what to tell you, Daco. I'm also not sure about what I'm doing.

"This war changed all of us…

"Hold on a sec, here's my wife at the door. Dijana, I'm talking to Daco on the phone - do you want to talk to him?"

I hear angry footsteps cross the floor and a voice, which painfully reminds me of something far too familiar:

"Fuck you and Daco! I had enough of you two in Sarajevo! Beep… beep… beep…"

I didn't have a chance to ask Mirsad how his wife is doing.

Endnotes

Šadrvan - A local bar in Sarajevo.

fate - The original word used here is *nafaka* which is a Turkish loan word meaning a cosmic fate.

papci - Slang for uncultured trashy people.

Egipat - Famous patisserie in Sarajevo.

Korzo - Another local bar.

raja - Bosnian word for your people, who transcend beyond just friendship and community.

Addict

Last Friday I went to the store with my cousin to buy grape leaves to make *japrak*. We picked the worst day at the worst hour, six in the evening when everyone is coming home from work and is shopping for the weekend and the following week.

The lines were stretching into infinity, and in front of us some granny miscalculated and overstuffed her cart with more than she could afford, and now she was faced with the hard task of deciding what to put back: a bag of chips or roll of toilet paper.

"Fuck the *japrak*," I say, annoyed, to my cousin and in that same moment I catch the glance of a guy who is standing next to us in line.

"Where are you from, *raja*?"

"From Sarajevo, and you?"

"Same."

He extends his hand to us, and with a smile he begins:

"I am Atif. Atif Abazović."

The name sounds familiar to me, and the guy seems like someone I might remember: the way his eyes smile, because you can't see his mouth through his thick mustache, the way he adjusts his glasses on his too-big nose.

The feeling is mutual, because he swears he knows me from "somewhere." We leave the store and we invite him for a drink across the street. He agrees, even though he says he stopped drinking a long time ago:

"A year before the Olympics I ended up in the hospital. I didn't just end up there; that year I drank with such ferocity that if you filled a pool with all of the brandy, *mastika*, *loza*, *zvekanac*, and *Vlahovac* - you'd have a hard time swimming across it. At that time, all I ate were hot dogs from a grill located near the high school, in total less hot dogs than fingers I had on my hand. That's when I stopped."

My cousin and I order Martell, and he orders a pitcher of beer.

We stare and he explains:

"Beer isn't a drink - beer is food. Do you know that in every beer there is a sip of milk and a bite of meat?"

And even that sounds familiar to me, and everything else he's talking about: professors from the high school, the crew from Sports Club FIS, bartenders from Old Istra, chicks from Park Cafe, hustlers from Bulevar... it's like him and I had one parallel life, but we never met, we just saw each other in passing, walked by each other in the same bar bathrooms, sat in the same rows in the same theaters, cheered at the same matches, rode the same tram…

"What do you do now, Atif?"

He lights a cigarette (again, with a familiar motion), deeply, deeply inhales the smoke, tops off his beer, wipes his mustache with the back of his hand, looks me in the eye and says:

"I'm healing myself. Unsuccessfully. It's been five years since I've abstained from Sarajevo, and even if I had been on the needle my whole life, by now I would have cleaned up, but I can't quit Sarajevo, even if my life depends on it. Sometimes it seems like it died in me, that I finally got rid of it, but the littlest thing, a familiar voice on the phone, a name in the paper, a dream, stirs it all up again in me, enough that I simply go crazy from desire, that… that… that I don't even know what…"

We silently drink, and I know (from my own experience) that the cruelest thing I could ask is:

"Well, why don't you go back?"

We part ways and we promise each other that we'll stay in contact.

If God wills it, as I always add.

Last night I called my cousin and I asked him if he has Atif's address or phone number, and he says he doesn't remember an Atif that we met at the store and went to get a drink with.

I tell him I'm not crazy, and he again repeats that I must be confused, that I was with someone else that day because he was working until late, he didn't go out after work, he watched basketball on TV…

Now I'm sitting here remembering how Atif didn't buy anything at the store that day (so why the fuck was he in line?) and I wonder if it's possible that I dreamed of Atif Abazović?

Or did Atif dream of me?

Endnotes

japrak - Stuffed grape leaves.

mastika, loza, zvekanac, and Vlahovac - An assortment of cheap local spirits.

Your People Are Your People

Jim Timony, my social worker, went to Nebraska to defend his PhD, so therefore next week I don't have to go to my mandatory session of repentance and spinning lies that a dog bribed with butter wouldn't even lick:

"Have you ever hit anyone?"

"Who? Me? What are you insinuating?"

"Did your father beat you as a child?"

"He beat me the shit out of me." (That's a justification that always works, even if I had slaughtered two people in broad daylight, they'd just pat me on the shoulder understandingly and let me go home, to work, to clean the bathrooms, to flip the burgers, to wash the dishes, to pack the fucking shirts, which all boils down to the same thing - i.e. that I work and pay taxes. But, under the condition that I'm an American like this...) The Christmas rush is over, and in the factory where I work, there are no more jobs for the seasonal workers, so I'm "on leave." I had a ton of overtime hours last month, and I got a Christmas bonus in the amount of a week's worth of pay, so I can get by for a bit.

Last night my friend Mujo called me from Florida. He's drunk and fed up with everything: "Today at the store, I'm lugging bags to some asshole's trunk, when I see a license plate from

Wisconsin. I tell him I have a friend, Daco, in Wisconsin, and he looks at me like I'm a piece of garbage and says: Let's go kid, I don't have all day here. Listen to him, calling me kid, I could have been his dad. I can't take it anymore, Daco - everything makes me sick."

"Are you working this weekend?

"I could but I don't want to."

"I'll drop by one of these days for a drink."

"You're fucking with me?"

"I haven't destroyed anyone in rummy in a while..."

In the off season, a Greyhound bus round-trip is just fifty-six dollars, and the trip to Tampa takes two days. Since I already have experience with fascist drivers, who prohibit any alcohol, I sip whisky from a liter of Coca-Cola and I'm off to see my friend, who escorted me out of Sarajevo five years ago, which was the last time I saw him.

I'm sitting in the Coral Bar in Tampa, Florida and everyone is looking at me like I'm crazy because I have boots on my feet, corduroy pants, a shirt and a heavy jacket (Canadian down) thrown over the back of my chair, and outside it's over thirty degrees Celsius. Mujo said he would come pick me up in half an hour, but here I am three beers later and he's still not here, and the kind bartender is giving me the phone again...

Dubravka, Mujo's wife, says to me that he left over half an hour ago, and being the idiot that he is, he probably got lost... On the other end of the bar is some old, burned out drunk and I know (because I'm a magnet for morons) that he'll eventually acknowledge me.

"I'm disgusted by most of humanity; I fucked 2,500 women, bet on 12,500 horse races, I drank a Lake Michigan's worth of alcohol, published twelve books... And you, you little pussy, what have you done with your life?"

The bartender says:

"Hey, Charles, that's enough..." but I interrupt.

"It's OK. Get the man a drink, whisky and water, on my tab," because on that unshaven face, full of deep wrinkles, that only pain can dig, unkempt, gray hair, clear blue eyes, I recognize something - *Vratnik, Bistrik, Marindvor, Korzo and Istra, Buffet San, Šetaliste, Plavi Podrum and Hamam Bar, Grad and Markinov Bar* - in one word: *raja.*

"Cheers, asshole," I tell him. "I missed out on 2,500 women, fucked up 12,500 horses, stole hundreds of books, I have two kids - there, that's what I've done with my life."

A smile sparkled in his eyes:

"Sandy, get the little pussy a drink on me."

"Thanks, old pussy."

"You know..." he begins, but I cut him off:

"I don't, but don't bother me, for God's sake"

(I was already worried that Mujo, the idiot, wasn't coming - but not because something could have happened to him - but rather because I'd have to spend money on a cab to his house.)

At that moment Mujo walked in: the same as always, just tanner, like he spent two summers in Ulcinj.

"Well, where have ya been, *ustašice*! You haven't even been in town for half an hour and you already know the biggest drunkards."

We hug and kiss, slobbering all over each other, and we cry, the few people of the American public in the bar are confused by the cacophony of Bosnian: "Fuck your mother's pussy... Eeeh, fuck your dad... You old whore... You fag... You stupid monkey... You idiotic jerk... Old moron... Motherfucker..." - all of our warm expressions of care and love. After we knocked all that out, I said:

"Sandy, get us a drink - what do you want, Mujo? One for Charles too." Mujo says, "Don't, Dubravka will be worried..."

"Don't worry, I called her already... Sandy, would you be so kind as to give me the telephone once more?"

Mujo calls his wife and tells her that we're having a drink and then coming home, I hear in Dubravka's voice, full of joy: "Fine, but please don't say that you're only going to stay for a bit with Daco, because with him you can't just stay for a bit."

Charles wants, little by little, to finish the thought that got stuck in his head half an hour ago:

"You know..."

"Sure, tell me!"

"You know, boy, you should take up writing."

"Thank you, Charles. I'll think about it."

***

After the fifth drink, Mujo and I leave the bar, and I ask him:

"How did you, this much of an idiot, luck out on a wife like Dubravka?"

Mujo looks at me with total non-understanding:

"Dubravka isn't my wife - she's my *raja*."

The years haven't changed Dubravka at all, she's the same as always - light-hearted and airy like a snowflake, with the same shine in her eyes and the same smile - truly as if only good things have happened to her in life.

But, on the other hand, I barely knew Dubravka and Mujo's son Zlaja: he just about has reached his father in height (which isn't that hard to do), he filled out, no resemblance to the little rascal that I saw last in Sarajevo.

He tells me he remembers me, and I believe him, then he asks me how my daughter Nevena is.

"She's good. She's already a big girl," but now I'm making things up because how can I tell him that I don't know, that I haven't seen my own daughter for eight months since I divorced my wife. We sit on the porch and we exchange information about our people: Rambo is in Australia, and Tule and Jolić,

Dubravka is also in America - we're both in contact with both of them; Tiho and Goro are in Canada, Bambi in Germany, Bobo in Sweden, Mosto in Canada, our Hamić and Kile aren't here anymore, neither are Mando or Bego…

We don't bring up the war, as if it was some bad dream, instead we recall every party at Hamić's store, card games at Mujo's house, poker at mine, the names of every waitress and waiter in the city, and while the empty beer cans pile up on the table we say to each other more and more:

"Look at what they did to us, what they did to us, motherfuckers…"

Dubravka made tripe (upon my request, because I had been craving it in America), and then she joins us. She asks me about the reasons for my divorce from Dijana, and I start with some overwrought vagueness, of course, putting all the blame on my ex, but Mujo cuts me off:

"*Rakija*, man, *rakija*!"

I can't not agree with him, and Dubravka says:

"I don't know, but she was always very dear to me," and there starts an awkward silence that's only remedied by the sound of a beer can opening and the clicking flint of a lighter.

It's already late, Dubravka works early in the morning, and neither Mujo nor I can drink as much as before, so I go to bed and I beg Dubravka to leave the lights on because I wouldn't want to piss in their pantry in the middle of the night…

I wake up with the worst hangover of my hangover-rich life. I can't shake the hiccups - not even beer is helping.

Mujo soon joins me and asks me:

"What did you, for heaven's sake, do with that detergent?"

"What detergent?"

"The one in the bags that were on the table in the kitchen?"

Slowly the film starts to replay: I got up at some point in the night, reached the kitchen, saw some bags with pictures of lemons on them and figured they were powdered lemonade, poured a couple of them into a pitcher and mixed it with water… It turns out those were advertising samples of a new detergent, "with lemon scent," that Mujo took from the supermarket where he works - that explains my heavy hangover.

Mujo asks me if I want breakfast, and I tell him I can't on an empty stomach and I open another beer…

Now we speak soberly: our plans for the future, life in America, life in Sarajevo…

"I don't know, Mujo," I say, "my only plan for now is to not die, still… Otherwise, I can't come to terms with the idea of ending up a cook in America… You know after the death of my father, a thousand times it happened that, at the post office, at the bank, with porters, when I took out my ID card, that someone would say: Ey, you're Vlatko's son, and my heart would be THIS BIG… I keep thinking, God willing, one day, when Nevena or maybe Vesna come to Sarajevo, that they'll look at their passports and say, "Ey, you're Daco's…" I don't know… I don't know…"

"Want me to show you the city?" asks Mujo.

"Eh, I don't give a fuck, they're all the same," I reply not even a little warmly, not because of Mujo, but because of my mindless attempt with this fifty six dollar trip, to try to return to the past and I almost miss my monotonous, murderous job, my bleak room, my never-ending lining up games of solitaire in solitude, unfamiliar pictures stuck on the TV, left by my Algerian friend Farida, Jim Timony and his washing of (my) brain…

Every decision I have made in my life has filled me with regret, and with that burden I sit on a bus and go back to "my Madison."

***

Before I left, my Lin, a Taiwanese girlfriend, warned me to beware of Koreans, and that they're the worst people on Earth -

how can I tell her that "they" all look the same to me?

In the foyer of the building where I live there is a TV, and a Chicago Bulls game is about to start. However, some chick came earlier and is watching some bullshit soap operas. Dave, a Korean, gets up and changes the channel; she protests, and I, "Gentleman Jim," tell the Korean to fuck off and I switch the channel back, not because I want to watch it, but because maybe I can glean something from the chick… That shit ends quickly and I turn the channel back to the Bulls; at halftime I go to the hall, the Korean is following me… and there, he knocks me out, not with Tae Kwon Do, Karate, Jiu Jitsu, but with a classic punch!

On Thursday, I show up to my meeting with a black eye, and the first thing I have to explain is if I had some sort of conflict this last week.

I lie and say I slipped at work and I hit the edge of a table. Even though he doesn't believe me, Jim Timony advises that I sue the employer, and I lie further and say it was my fault, because I didn't immediately wipe the floor where I had spilled something…

Rick is driving me home. He is the new (just five-six weeks) guy "in class" and is on probation because he stomped out his half-brother, a drug addict who was extorting money from their mother. He hates drug addicts and he doesn't show any remorse for what he did and he always says that he'd do it again if it happened again, if he had to.

During our drive I tell him what actually happened and then I go to the Nitty Gritty, across the street from my house, for drinks.

At the bar, Dave, the Korean, is laughing at me.

"That's the asshole that laid me out," I say to Rick, and he coldly answers:

"I don't give a shit."

***

Rick hasn't shown up for two meetings, so I ask Jim Timony what happened to him.

"Sadly he went back to prison. He broke parole - he beat up some guy from Korea at the Nitty Gritty. It's near your apartment."

"Do you know which prison he's in?"

"In Bloomington, I would imagine. Why are you asking?"

"Just because…"

P.S. I'm ashamed that I still haven't visited Rick.

Endnotes

ustašice - Catholic Croatian Fascist front that was active during WWII.

The Other Side of the Coin

I know that to the readers of what I'm writing everything makes less and less sense and they, with good reason, ask themselves after they've read my stories: fuck this guy, is there anything good in that goddamn America?

250 million and counting people live there and no one complains as much as HIM?!

HE, who was born on some street in Sarajevo, one-room with no bathroom, with a squat toilet (that he had to share with the neighboring kids); slept in the same room with his father and mother, uncle and aunt Ana (grandpa and grandma slept in the kitchen, on an ottoman); ate meat only on Sundays; the wood stove which heated him as well, was the only "kitchen appliance," and on which was prepared for him his, to this day hated, grits.

HE, who served as the favorite food for indestructible fleas and bedbugs, which sprung up from the wooden floor covered with tarps, and walls that were last painted maybe a week before the arrival of Franz Ferdinand in Sarajevo.

HE, who wore his first pair of jeans (Super Rifle) when he finished eighth grade with good grades, he who from his first year of high school (when he became independent, which is to say became alone) only had gym shorts and a shirt for pajamas and underwear... and so on and so forth, and let's not forget an important and perhaps only detail that he wore as his proof of identity, a bottle opener around his neck?

HE???!!!

HE is whining?! HE is complaining?! FOR HIM nothing can be good?! As if America has no other purpose or job other than to make his life truly unbearable?!

That's why I'm trying to uncover the other side of the coin, to amend this undesirable impression.

There must be a million good things in America!

First of all, like their Bill of Rights:

"All people are created equal!"

There is no bigger truth than that in the world! (I guess, they haven't heard of when my pal Mirsad Kaukčija had a kid, and he got a call from the hospital that Sabina was OK, and that he's a father, and he - I think he was working at Bosna Cars - ditched work, ordered everyone, known and unknown, drinks at Kvarner, and another, and another, to not drag on... when at some point they asked him; "Well, Mise, is it a daughter or a son?" And he replies: "It is"; "What do you mean, man, it is? Is it a weenie or piss hole?"; "I told you it is; it's a daughter or it's a son - it's gonna be something either way.")

It doesn't say, obviously, in the American Constitution what happens later: will the mother, that same day, leave the hospital and rush to work at McDonald's, to pick strawberries in California, to sew shirts in Wisconsin, to pick up trash in New York, or will she call a conference for the press to announce the birth of her ilk, and then go dip her pussy on the beach in Florida - like she has her whole life - because the Constitution says, and let me simplify, that everyone is the master of their own luck.

It is a big Constitutional right that everyone can bear arms. (The fact that Bosnians can isn't mentioned in that regard because the creators of America hadn't even heard of us, even though we were a kingdom and existed some measly 600 years before them.) Then, every American has a right to vote. (Is there a bigger right on Earth than the right to vote, ask my American friends, drunk off luck and free beer that is given out at voting locations? I didn't want to hurt their deep feelings of patriotism and tell them that in our country you can vote whenever, however many times you want, wherever you want, under whatever name you so desire…)

Eric Clapton (even though he's English) is something that makes me happy about America. I listen to his new hit "My Father's Eyes," I look at him, really nothing, ugly, bald, bearded, and he reminds me of my friend Goran Krnet, who is now in Canada… When I remember Gora, I can't help but remember Lilo, who is in Sarajevo… The fact that a man like Lilo still walks this Earth is a big source of joy for me.

Jack Nicholson won an Oscar again and I'm happy for him because I heard he's a great guy and I'm sure we'll get along splendidly when we meet each other.

But the best thing about America is when I call my daughter Nevena, and an even better thing is when she calls me - and I cuddle the phone and I smile like an idiot, even half an hour after getting off the phone.

I don't have the words to express my happiness when I talk to my three-year-old American daughter Vesna, when we spend ten minutes repeating to each other only: "I love you, child" and "I love you, dad"... in our language.

Could HE possibly wish for more?!

He Looks at Me Like a Beast, Because I Am One

Sparse snowflakes, as if they hesitated to fall to the ground. That was the reason that I didn't wait for the bus when I was coming back from work around midnight - about half an hour to the first open bar, a few drinks and then home.

Halfway there, the sky opened up and I entered the bar like a bank of snow. The rejoicing student body (happier now because of the soon-to-come Christmas break, not to mention that it was Friday), welcome me with: "Ho! Ho! It's Santa Claus..." which I didn't enjoy one bit, because they represented something I would never be, their youthful joy and energy were simply hurtful to someone who had spent the last eight hours washing dishes and had to pretend he was happy to have that job.

I do have to recognize that I did look like the butt of a joke, with my fully gray beard, that I let grow out of laziness, and my only shred of protection against the cruel winter wind, a second-hand windbreaker with a hood (that I still wear with pride).

There wasn't anything aggressive in their behavior, because to them I was a nobody.

Maybe that's the reason why I ordered an entire pitcher of beer, and with the careless bartender's question of "How many glasses?" I replied with "One, what did you think?"

Sitting next to me at the bar, guessing by appearance (in a light blue suit, with a silk tie and Italian shoes) a type that rarely ended up in a hole like this. He looked at me with interest, but not like how gays usually look at other gays. He asked for a light, and I pushed my lighter across the bar; he then asked where I was from, and I regretted that I ordered a whole pitcher, but it didn't even cross my mind to leave it half-drunk because what's paid for is paid for.

He took a business card out of his pocket, apologizing politely: "Phil Constantino," I remember it well.

For some, only known to him, reason, he asked how old I am. I answered (forty at that time).

"You're kidding?" he asked me.

"Why would I joke about that - I guess I know how fucking old I am?!"

"I can't believe it - I'm forty-seven."

Even though he was dead drunk, I wouldn't have guessed he was older than thirty.

"Wanna bet… on a drink?"

(He was drinking gin, Tanqueray and tonic to be exact, and I calculated that would be about the same price). But he insisted…

"Fifty dollars?!"

I had nothing left to do except take my ID card out.

Without a word he took out fifty dollars, ordered himself another gin and tonic, paid with another fifty dollar bill, told the bartender that he didn't need the change - luckily she didn't hear him - he was blabbing about his soy business, and then, before he finished his drink, had enough and left…

Forty-five dollars was left on the bar, and with the speed of a rattlesnake I swiped it, and left a full glass of beer to go home, but not without the anxiety that I would hear behind me the official, very unfriendly voice of a police officer:

"Excuse me, sir?" (Which would mean that I'd have to blow him because I was still on parole.)

I sat in my room, listened to a cassette of the *Indexi*, played solitaire, watching the beautiful curtain of snow, and remembered one long-ago night, when I was walking back from Sloga with Oljo, when we looked back, and down Kranjčevićeva only our footsteps in the snow; and my home is warm, warm...

It was too late (or early) to call my daughter Nevena, but, because it was almost her birthday, I firmly decided that in the morning I would go visit her and we could decide what she would want me to get her for her birthday...

***

I sit at the Silver Dollar bar, where the bartender, regardless of the fact that every month I give him half of my pay, always contemptuously stares...

I'll have just one screwdriver to fix myself, call a taxi, and then I'm going to see Nevena... I'm going to have just one more...

Into the bar walks a guy with a big glass jar - like one used for pickling, but in it two rattlesnakes: he puts it on the bar and bets (five dollars) that no one will be able to keep their hand on the jar when the snake strikes from behind the glass; the glass was thick enough to withstand an atom bomb, and the people with their confident smiles pressed their palms against the glass, and then, when she attacked, they all reflexively pulled back...

Some of them, in disbelief, spit in their "sissy" hands, and then he came up to me and I asked for a raised bet of fifty dollars.

"Why not?" he says, not knowing that I would actually prefer that the glass was as thin as a sheet of cellophane, to end everything, because I know I'm already drunk and that today I won't go see my beautiful daughter.

Everyone huddles around me - my hand doesn't move.
He counts out fifty dollars and looks at me like I'm a beast.
Because I am one.

Endnotes

the Indexi - Sarajevan rock band.

The Night They Drove Sarajevo Down

John has been a cook his entire life. He's balding and gray. He looks like he's in his seventies. Today I found out it's only his fiftieth birthday.

Namely, today, when we got to work at the Holiday Inn, there was a bouquet of flowers and a balloon with *Happy Birthday*, a card for his fiftieth birthday…

John acts surprised, he winks at me with his blue eyes and he tries to put on a sneaky smile: "I know who could have sent this."

Shivers went down my spine, because in that second I realized John, who doesn't even have a dog or a cat, sent himself the flowers and balloon. I wished him a happy birthday and saw myself in some ten years doing the same thing and tricking some other immigrant with "I know who could have sent this to me."

After work I invited him for a drink. He wavers, and then I remember I didn't use the right phrase "I'll buy you a drink," so I correct myself, and he of course agrees.

We walk past the Civic Center (something like the Radnički, Đuro Đaković, or Templ, but now I don't know what it's called) and I see a poster for a Joan Baez concert: tickets are thirty dollars and in my pocket I only have twenty-six.

I apologize to John that the drinks have to wait for another occasion, and that I want to go to the concert and if he has a pen and piece of paper…

I write "Dear Miss Baez, I know you don't remember me and can't remember me. We met on the occasion of your concert in 1993 in Sarajevo, I was in the company of Professor Zdravko Grebo. You don't know how much joy your visit brought me and my fellow citizens. I would like to give you my warmest thanks and to see and hear from you again."

John is looking at me like a madman while I hand the message to the porter. (It turns out, later, that the porter is a refugee from Hungary - if he had been an American he probably would have wiped his ass with it.)

After a few minutes he comes back and asks me how many tickets I need. I ask John if he wants to go with me, and he looks at me like I hit him with an Allah the Most Sublime.

"Two," I said to the Hungarian and I stretched out my hand to introduce myself: "My name is Robert Zimmerman."

He was called Ladislav Jonas.

John stays by the bar and I go behind the stage. Joan Baez acts like she recognizes me. We hug and kiss. Her guitarist tells me that Gino Banana is in Seattle and gives me his number.

The concert is about to begin and Joan tells me we must see each other after. She asks if I'm staying backstage or if I'll go out into the crowd….

I'm going into the crowd and they take me to the first row…

Joan's angelic voice makes me feel like I'm floating, as if everything is normal in my life, as if I'm no longer human waste, as if this "affair" (how some call this nameless horror in Bosnia) never even happened…

The line up is: Amazing Grace, Diamonds and Rust, The Ballad of Joe Hill…

And then Joan announces:

"Now, a song for our friend from Sarajevo, Dario…"

She sings "The Night They Drove Old Dixie Down" and changes the lyrics to "Sarajevo Down."

I'm no longer floating, but rather flying through the auditorium, my head is hitting the ceiling, the walls, I'm crying at the beauty and the horror at the same time…

After the concert Joan is in the greenroom giving out autographs, and John and I wait for the frenzy to settle down a bit.

The bartender, Gwen, asks if I'm actually from Sarajevo and brusquely fills our glasses; John doesn't say a word about it, because in his life as a line cook, this is the most exciting night so far.

The crowd breaks up and I beg Joan to sign a picture for my daughter Vesna… She asks how old she is.

"She was born in May."

"You know, Dario, what happened to me recently. After a concert, a teenage girl came up to me, and I, quite happily, assumed that the younger generations are still listening to me! That's when she says, "Can you make it out to my grandmother?""

I ask her if she's interested in reading some stories that I wrote in English and she gives me her address and phone number so that I definitely send them to her.

I invite her for a nightcap somewhere else, because the green room is already clearing out.

She apologizes and says she's sorry:

"Another time," she says, as if running over to Malibu is like running over to *Sirano*.

She asks me:

"What are you going to do now?"

"Nothing," I say and I ask Gwen the bartender where she lives…

Endnotes

Sirano - Old, well-known cafe in Sarajevo.

All These (New) Years

Now, as I sit in my madhouse, with my wonderful madmen, who don't wish any ill on me, only expect good from me, I remember that tonight is December 31st, and, allegedly, I should celebrate the New Year.

With whom? With what?

I still haven't introduced the practice of hiding beer in the dog house, and without even undressing, I stretch out in bed and wish to myself that 1999 will be a better, much better year for me… and I think about all the other previous New Year's nights…

SARAJEVO, BiH, 1969.

For the new opening of *Skenderija* there was a "rock-marathon," and me, a little runt, fourteen years old, like Alice in Wonderland, overjoyed that I had a 5,000 dinar bill in my pocket, the feeling of freedom in my heart, I emptied plastic cups of beer, listened to Čičak, watched Širaz Muftić paint a surreal mural, "danced" on the disco club floor, proudly waved my long hair and was lonely in the crowd. In the morning there was something to see: over a meter of snow fell. From Skenderija to my house (some five hundred meters away) took over two hours to walk through the mounds. My grandma was waiting for me with warm palms for my frozen face: "You should have called us, we were worried about you," and my grandpa snorted: "I'm missing 5,000 from my wallet. Do you, kid, know anything about that?"

Happy New Year, grandma and grandpa!

SARAJEVO, BiH, 1970-1989.

It seems like they were all the same: wild drunkenness in the apartments of someone's wealthy parents, who, for the holiday, had gone away to the mountains on Jahorina, inevitable Russian salad, squeaky record players and scratched records, short-lasting gasps ("What's your problem, are you crazy?") in side rooms, never-ending phone calls at midnight, fights and make-ups, love and jealousy, the smell of vomit in the bathroom, the sour smell of open and undrunk bottles of wine, heavy, virginal hangovers, piss-poverty and depression, because everyone now will go home, and me in Korzo, making out with the waitress Rada, she'll cut up some roast that she brought from Han-Pijesak, and I'll nap in the corner, alone...

Happy New Year, Rada!

SARAJEVO, BiH, 1989.

No more morning benders, those empty conversations: "I swear, I don't want to go anywhere,"; "For all I fucking care, everyday's New Year's"; chipping in for drinks and meze, arguments with drunks, how much to spend on alcohol, and how much on other shit... I'm a married man, and eleven days ago my daughter was born: I'm no longer alone! I sit next to Nevena's crib, and the spirit of love fills our apartment; every once in a while I bend down and uncover her or cover her a bit, just to make sure she's there, that the little creature that made me a dad is living....

I would like to endlessly make love to my wife but she says

she hasn't healed from the delivery.

Regardless: Happy New Year, Nevena!

SARAJEVO BiH, 1990.

A few days ago I bought a tie from my friend Nijaz Dizdarević Bunjo, and then I realized that I had nothing to wear it with, so I was forced to buy my first suit of my life.

For New Year's I was a guest on TV Channel 3. I was glowing, horribly sober: the host is pushing me to talk about my "bohemian" life (which means my misery and poverty), and I reply that that's all behind me, that I have just two women in the world that I love: my wife and daughter.

Through a yellow, thick, foam-like fog I impatiently return home anticipating my wife's commentary…

She said she overslept.

And then she falls asleep again.

My apartment is decorated like the Cathedral and I'm waiting for midnight to put on the John Lennon song "We wish you a Merry Christmas and Happy New Year"... but Dijana wakes up and her normally lovely face is distorted by malice, "Do you always have to play the fool?"

Suddenly that respectable tie strangles me, and because, again alone, I end up at the *Dom Pisaca* where nobody needs me…

Happy New Year, Dijana!

SARAJEVO, BiH, 1991.

No information.

SARAJEVO, BiH, 1992.

Wiped from memory.

SARAJEVO, BiH, 1993.

I had nothing to celebrate.

PARDEVILLE, WI, USA, 1994.

This was supposed to be the New Year's of our new life, in a new world, but, despite the best intentioned wishes of our hosts, Ivan and Marija Rabotski, it'll be a year of bundled love and hate that will come undone in the end.

Even though I am alone again: Happy New Year, Ivan and Marija.

DODGEVILLE, WI, USA, 1995.

My American woman is in her fifth month of pregnancy. We got an invite from our friends, Nenad and Indira. The American woman brushed off how much we can drink, but she was envious because during pregnancy she wasn't drinking.

When, early in the morning, we came back home, we made love frantically, as if we suspected that she and I would soon end up alone.

Happy New Year, Nenad and Indira.

DODGEVILLE, WI, USA, 1996.

I'm coming back from work at the factory: New Year's Eve has long passed - it's already 1am. The house is decorated like the Cathedral; I take a beer out of the fridge, I bend down on the bed of my daughter Vesna, I take in her sweet breath. I'd kiss her but I don't want to wake her.

I sat in the "living room" and very quietly I put on the John Lennon record; "We wish you a Merry Christmas and Happy New Year..."

From the bedroom I hear: "Turn off the music, you maniac. I have to work tomorrow."

Happy New Year, Janette!

MADISON, WI, USA 1997.

I sit in my room, listening to an *Indexi* song, and I remember how you once told me, when I asked you why you like them,

you said: "Dad, when I listen to your Indexi, I dream in color."
Happy New Year, Vesna, happy everything, my dear bunny.

SARAJEVO, BiH, 1999.
It is still not known.

Endnotes

wonderful madmen - Dario worked briefly at a mental institution as an orderly.

Skenderija - A cultural and sports center.

Dom Pisaca - Writer's Club in Sarajevo.

Incest

Never quit a job until you've found another one, rule number one in America! I had forgotten it, so for some time I was "on standby," and being broke in America is probably one of the worst fates that can befall a person. The first of the month was approaching, that dark day when rent is due, and I only have $34 in my pocket - I'm $241 away from being homeless.

After a few unsuccessful tries, I found an ad for a Turkish restaurant looking for a cook. The pay would be $7.50 an hour (a whole dollar more than at my previous job at the Holiday Inn), and what's more important is that it's about five minutes away from my apartment. (There were a bunch of jobs, but I needed to have a car, which for me is a pipe dream.)

I go to the interview and it turns out the restaurant isn't going to be open until the end of the month. Either way, I got the job.

The owners were Mehmet and Veli. I helped them with the final touches, but as it always goes, something goes wrong and the opening is pushed back.

In the meantime, I became friends with Veli, and he offered for me to live with him, because his girlfriend went to Brazil for study-abroad, so he has an empty room. It turns out that a

"Turkish kitchen" has nothing to do with what we eat and make in the *Čaršija*. Can you imagine - they've never heard of *khash*!?

Veli and Mehmet worked from dusk till dawn. They only took breaks between one and five in the afternoon, between lunch and dinner, when there wasn't any business, so I was left alone in the restaurant.

That's how I bumped into some sad-eyed bum, which was the only reason I bought a pin in the shape of the American flag from him. He handed me a paper saying he's deaf and that, allegedly, all his income goes to an association for the deaf.

I was so bored, I waved him over with a *džezva* (as if I could have a good chat with him), and he agreed with a nod of his head.

He's sitting and drinking coffee: takes a bite of a cube of sugar, sips, and at that, taps his foot along to the rhythm of the music: something lights before my eyes, so I walk up behind him, and in our language I say:

"So, how's it going in America?"

He jumps, like a snake just bit him.

It turns out he's from Sarajevo, that he's from Sutjeska Street, from Koreja, the poor "slum" across the street from the Second Gymnasium.

He tells me in the boonies, in smaller places, where people are more generous and bigger patriots than in cities, he can get $150 a day, but there's also a bigger chance of getting caught by the cops. That happened once, and he served time for six months.

We say goodbye and wish each other luck with everything. He leaves, I lift up the tray with the *džezva* and *fildžan* and under - fifty dollars!

My eyes tear up with feelings of happiness and sadness.

However, that wasn't the only encounter from our neck of the woods I had that day.

Namely, that day I had some sort of literary event at a

bookshop, so I dressed up: black jeans, black leather jacket, white shirt and a tie, and with how much I had significantly reduced my drinking at Veli's, I actually looked quite acceptable. Now, before the dinner, I'm sitting at the Angelic Brewery, drinking a dark Irish stout, with my books spread out in front of me (I brought them in the hopes that at the bookshop I'll run into the Director of Penguin Books and that he'll give me a contract for publishing, and that's the same as if I was wishing I would win the lottery), I'm rolling a cigarette with a rolling machine, when a girl comes up to me, twenty-something years old and fascinated with my machine, as if it's the most recent technological wonder, and she begs me to roll one for her too.

She notices the books on the table and asks me what language they're in.

"Serbo-Croatian," I say and expect her to stare at me blankly as if I said Sanskrit, but she exclaims:

"For real? My grandma is from Croatia. What are they about?"

"I don't know. I haven't read them - I only wrote them," I reply, not without a hint of vanity.

Now she doesn't believe me anymore, so I turn to a page with my picture on it. I'm ten years younger, but still recognizable.

Her name is Prudence Crnkovic and she studies IT.

"What?"

"Crnkovic," she repeats.

I tell her that's the maiden name of my grandmother and we laugh at "what a small world" it is, and I make up in my head, that in her facial features, in her thin, refined nose, semi-ironic smile, long fingers, I recognize the memories of a person I love immeasurably.

She's sorry she doesn't have time to go to the literary event with me, but that she would really like to see each other again; she leaves her phone number and says that it's best to call after

7pm because she's in class all day.

The next few days I'm torn on whether I should call her, but I don't want to come on too strong, so I let the invite rest for a week.

I could have expected a million things, that she would say: "Dario? Which Dario?"; "Get lost, moron!"; "You have the wrong number"; "I'm sorry, but I really just don't have time," but that she would agree to a meeting, and at that add "Do you have anything against my mother coming along?" is something I couldn't have dreamt even in my darkest nightmare.

"Well, of course not," I reply and I feel like someone is playing a practical joke on me.

I'm changing my mind, I wouldn't make it to the meeting - I'd just spend money for no reason, but nonetheless, I decide to go…

What do I see: the most beautiful woman I've seen in a while. Forty years old, but she has totally gray, short hair, the bluest eyes, long legs and the stature of a model, a warm handshake and a dazzling smile.

"I am Mary. Pru's mother. Nice to meet you."

Same for me, how could it not be, you have no idea how happy I am that we met…

After the death of her husband, four years ago, she switched back to her maiden name; she works as a tour guide - and just now she's preparing for a tour of the South and she's surprised by my knowledge of the Civil War, like the fact that the general who organized the Buffalo Soldiers, the first black regiment, was from Wisconsin…

Prudence's boyfriend came to pick her up and they went to the movies, but I didn't even notice… At the end of the evening, which went by like the snap of a finger, I offer to order her a taxi, but she tells me she lives nearby and that she'd rather walk.

It's a warm summer evening and we walk arm in arm. She invites me for coffee, but I turn it down, pretending that I have to wake up early the next day for work, but really, I'm shitting bricks.

I don't know. Maybe that night I came off as a loser, maybe I could have committed "incest" but, either way, I don't regret it, because it remained an eternal, steadfast friendship… and nobody can take that away from me.

Endnotes

Čaršija - The old Turkish market of Sarajevo.

džezva - Pot for making Turkish coffee.

fildžan - Small cup for drinking Turkish coffee.

God's Finger and Fist

If Slobodan Kovačević is still alive, I could meet him on the corner of Kralja Tomislava and Džidžikovac, he'd be bouncing his enormous body from one foot to the other, rubbing his hands together, and telling me about myself; my entire genealogy, where I was born and where I lived, and even my phone number.

(For those who don't know, Slobo was a Sarajevan legend, one who was, how Indigenous Americans would say, touched by the heavens, but we in Sarajevo would more simply say: loony.)

Unfortunately, they told me, he died over the summer and he looked exactly the same as he had for the last thirty years (the only difference was that he didn't know the genealogy of a lot of the people he ran into on the street), so now I'm not sure that I even exist or if I ever even did.

Especially when the stupid bureaucrats told me my *Matični Broj* didn't exist in the system, and they don't even have a file on me, and that my apartment had been considered abandoned since 1971 after the death of my father (OK, well, at least they recognized that I had a father).

I met Slobo's incarnation in Madison, in America, and he was called, which I will later learn, Sidney.

His territory was State Street - very similar to our Ferhadija, with a bunch of cafes and stores, street sellers, walkways and meeting places for students and slackers, beggars and businessmen, gays and lesbians, members of every sect…

Sidney was hard to classify in just one category; put aside the easily recognizable ones like "uniformed" businessmen, with their haughty, arrogant facial expressions and non-stop glances at their Rolexes (if you didn't know - time is money), but he wasn't like the regular beggars, who, rattling change in plastic yogurt cups, circle the streets in silence (because it's illegal for them to pay attention to passerbys) begging for their own piece of the American Dream.

So, he would stand, tapping his foot, in front of a glass vitrine full of cakes in a local cafeteria until someone would order him a coffee or an apple pipe, or tuck a dollar into his hand.

On the street he would stop people and quiz them about the winners of the Oscars, but he never had a problem with the police, because from behind his eyes, the color of unroasted coffee, radiated a gentleness and goodness.

On my way to an interview at an Italian restaurant "Botticelli," where the money was good, I tucked a five dollar bill in his hand for good luck and it paid off: I got a gentlemanly job, flexible work hours, plus, I got to split tips with the waitstaff.

That's how our "friendship" began. I would regularly, on my way home from work carrying a pack of beer, run into Sidney and pass a can into his hands, and he would, for example, ask me if I knew who won the Oscar in 1936 for Best Actress, etc.

He was always freshly shaved and the modest attire he wore was always clean and he never gave off any sense of misery, or that specific air of "damp" mold and decay, piss and alcohol, beans without meat, nicotine and rotten teeth, which, I guess, surrounds all unfortunates in this world, so it wasn't uncomfortable for me to sit with him every once in a while in some "garden" on the pavement, have a coffee and learn about how his father lives in Detroit and that he has paid for his accommodation at the YMCA for twelve years now - since the death of his mother, who he called "mommy."

I asked him how old he was (he looked like he was in his thirties), but he didn't know how to answer, because it seemed as though he only counted time since "mommy" died.

In school he had problems with dyslexia (if that's what it's called), which means that he never learned to read or write, and all the other tidbits of information about the Oscars he has memorized from video tapes. Why he (or his father) chose Madison, he wasn't able to tell me.

From what I could figure out, he was sent here by his stepmother ("A mild, but evil woman," as he describes her), who he, just as his father, loves and every year sends a Christmas card to - one that someone else wrote.

Anyways, one day I ran into him on the street, shining in brand new jeans, cowboy boots, with a bolo tie; he invites me for a drink at the most expensive place (Blue Marlin) in the city...

We sit in a real garden, with oleander and bougainvillea around us, and I don't even wonder to myself about the changes, because if it's normal that I haven't seen my daughter Nevena in eight months, then anything is normal to me.

He orders a beer for me and a coffee and (of course) an apple pie for himself, and I ask him why he isn't having a beer:

"I don't drink alcohol."

"And all those beers I gave you?"

"I didn't want to hurt your feelings, Dario, because you also are a lonely man. I would share them with the other "unfortunates" in the park." (Drunks, or here as they call them, winos.) He invites me to go with him to Oneida, a reservation with a casino, which isn't far from Madison - some sixty miles.

"Sidney, where'd the money come from?" I finally ask.

"My dad died."

I didn't go to the casino with Sidney, but a few days later I got the boot from work and went to Seattle, where in the newspaper a few months later I saw his picture and I read how at the Oneida Casino he managed to lose $80,000 within a month's time, and now he's suing (with a lawyer) the state, because as per his father's will, the inheritance should be paid out monthly instead of in a lump sum.

...Again, later, I read that he won; the money was returned to him and is now being paid out monthly.

I'm happy for Sidney, who God touched with his finger, but I ask myself, what will I, who owes America $15,000, do?

Saying God hit me with a fist won't fly at all in American courts.

Endnotes

Matični Broj - Yugoslav version of a Social Security Number.

El Niño in My Head

If I knew what was going on around me, I would know what I'm doing. I've lost all sense of time - what time even! - for seasons. Once there were four:

Spring, that is when I would, shuffling in front of my *raja*, be the first to take my shoes off and dare to walk barefoot down the street (although the soles of my feet hated it), and then in order to not fall behind, the others would follow and kick a ball in the park behind the Second Gymnasium; I picked hellebores and primrose along the banks of the Miljacka, crocus and galanthus in Gaj and would bring bouquets to my grandmother, and she would devoutly hold on to them, as if I had brought her the Holy Grail:

Summer was the end of school, trading report cards, some money from family for all A's (except a C for behavior), departures to the sea with my father, in Cavtat, where I hated him while he hit on German women, and I mindlessly and furiously threw a hook and line from the pier and couldn't wait to get back to my Sarajevo, where waiting for me was:

Autumn, I always hated school, but my dear friends: Ilija, Rile, Elo, Mirza, Mise, Ljupe..., more countless games of soccer and basketball in FIS and coming up:

Winter, when I would crazily descend down Dalmatinska on a homemade sled, could hardly wait for the New Year's party at Braco's, on the floor above me, with my old crew: Ogi, Čupo, Biban, Čedo...to be drunk not only off the obligatory Pearl of Fruškogorje, but also the feeling of importance from being in charge of playing on the Czech Supraphon records from Adam and Jane Birkin, imagining how divine it will be when I grow up and I kiss (on the mouth) their daughters, who are - from a realistic assessment actually ugly, if not average but looked like goddesses to me - a flash of bare breasts or ass made that winter feel like the hottest season; after that a traditional midnight match in a half-court, in the frozen garden of the Šetaliste, where we would slide, fall, laugh, Zlaja, Ranko, Mirko, Čuka, Slađo, Brdo, Kusta, Omer...when I wait for my upcoming birthday, not knowing that every coming year will bring me closer to this fifth season in which I now live: every day is the same to me, and I don't know if it's El Niño, or some other cosmic force, that my barren days, seasons (which I only recognize based on the clothing I'm wearing), turn into despair, (what a corny phrase) as if "I'm grasping for straws," and in fact grasping the telephone and calling Ljubljana, Ozrenka, who dumped me 19 years ago:

"Hey, it's me," she recognized my voice.

"Oh wow, you?"

"Well, you know, I wanted to ask you something... Actually I'm calling from Seattle, from America, I'm planning on coming back to Sarajevo, and I thought of stopping by to see you?"

"What did you want to ask me?"

"I almost forgot: Why did you, for god's sake, dump me?"

"Do you ever listen to yourself, Dario?"

"Yeah, well what?!"

"You're calling me after nineteen years: you don't ask how I am, if I'm married, if I have kids, what I'm doing, but you'd, just like that, drop by? Man, get it together!"

And there I got myself together. (But whenever I get myself

together, I fall apart.)

Everything that makes me happy brings me to tears.

"You're right, Ozrenka, I'm sorry, if that means anything to you... I just wanted to... It doesn't matter... Bye."

***

If anything, in my loneliness I have developed the skill to dream of only what I want, and that which I don't, I don't even recall.

I know that only an idiot dwells on the past, and that a smart man thinks about the future, and I lay down in bed, fully dressed, and I focus on dreaming of my kids, more their voices (because I have pictures), smell and touch, everything that I miss.

I wake up in a cold sweat; as if I was interrogated by some freaks...They sat behind heavy writing desks, in front of them piles of paper and heaps of graphite pencils, which they nonstop sharpened... In the background plays some unrecognizable music, and they ask me what nationality I am...

I dead seriously answer:

"A dead man. A member of the biggest nationality on Earth."

They shuffle the papers in front of themselves:

"That can't be. You are still alive."

***

The sun rose, and according to the calendar, it should be summer, but through the window I see snowflakes.

Is it El Niño in my head or can I not even dream anymore?

Sara, Mara, Dara from Drvar

It was once said: the things a broke person can come up with, a train couldn't even pull!

So like that: I'm coming home in the dead of night from my job in the factory, and tomorrow I have to go into my "honorary" job at a flower shop, where, you won't believe it, I have the very great responsibility of taking the thorns off roses.

It's not any kind of money, but that's why I have free Band-Aids and the right to swear to high heaven if I prick myself and to smoke, because I work outside.

Valentine's Day is approaching, so roses out the ass, and I, with the goofy smile of a half-idiot, get a thank you from my landlady:

"Good job, dario (I purposefully wrote my name with a lowercase letter, because, it's said in such a tone, with so much "emotion" and respect, that I, truly, feel like "d"), and I think about how I'll get rich in America:

Daco, man, leave the matches alone - that is the, I suppose, only useful thing you have learned in life: Fuck Kafka, Dostoevsky, Gogol, Maupassant: those were all big losers, fools, who if in their "rich" lives, bumped into hustlers like Šune, Očenaš, Činija or Fuko.... would bet on, again and again, the wrong cup.

...I know I can't explain this in English: "'*Sara, Mara, Dara from Drvar,* are looking for little Janko. Where are you, little Janko?" You don't know, for five thousand, and not you, Sir Jackass, and not you, not you..." but we'll think of something...

... The problem is the shill too; like if I had Ljupko... the best shill in the world; always dressed to the nines, with a silk scarf around his neck, he'd always carry an apple in his pocket, and when he'd notice a mark approaching, he'd ask him:

"Excuse me, do you happen to have a knife I can peel this apple with?"

The mark would take a knife out (usually a pocketknife from Visoko), and Ljupko would say to Očenaš:

"Get him now, Oko."

(Uh, fuck me, I poked myself!)

Eh, what a time that was: All the crews from class had their own idols - Musemić or Hasanagić, Vjećo Tolj or Nikola Plećaš, but my "gods" were the hustlers.

And even if I just "kept watch" and I didn't get a "full cut," I knew how to "earn" in a day my father's monthly salary.

One time my old man turned out my pockets and found a wad of cash; he asked me where I got it, and I told him that I'm the class treasurer, that I'm collecting money for a class trip; he went to my school to check they weren't crazy enough to trust me with money. I persistently denied that I was gambling (which was his assumption), so he stuffed the money into his own pocket and, most likely, took some skank out to dinner at Hotel Evropa.

But we gambled too. After a long day at work on the Boulevard, we usually went to Kovačić to Vito's, at Dva Ferala, and we played rummy.

The hustlers, even if they are over-the-top thieves, to me, from a better crowd, were pussies in rummy - I cleaned up with them, and they were proud of me, because I was the only one in our circle who made it to high school. They were confused by my report cards - especially by my A in English and Serbo-Croatian.

When I published my first poems in *Spektar* they threw me a real party.

This lasted for about a year and half, and then began a big purge and in the "process of a century," all the Sarajevan swindlers were picked up by the police.

The longest sentence was given to poor Fuko, who because he was so poor, couldn't hire a lawyer. (Later Fuko said: "I'm looking at my court-appointed lawyer, and he's writing, writing something… I lean over his shoulder to take a look, and he's drawing a black raven in his notebook… Eh, you're fucked, Fuko, I think to myself.")

I followed the cases until one day when the judge kicked me ("the little girl in the first row" - I had long hair back then) out of the courtroom.

That's how it all pissed out, but I found new idols and role models for myself, a different type of villain - Sarajevan writers…

(Ugh, I pricked myself on a thorn again.)

***

My biggest problem was finding a box of matches, because in America there aren't any - they all light up with Zippos, BICs, or those branded shitty matchbooks; however I manage to find "safety matches" in a specialized smoke shop. I buy a "Milka" chocolate (to not jinx it, because Fuko once told me that's the foil that makes the best balls).

I leave the chocolate for my daughter, and I make two balls: because I don't have a shill, I can't count on the basic trick (when you mix them up, you slip the ball under the middle box and push another one in), that's the draw, so I have to immediately go on "double duty" (you put two balls under two boxes, show one, immediately slip it out, and you don't even touch the box under which the other ball is), but you can only play that once or twice for big money.

I practiced a bit at home, and then I went to the Red Room, a beer hall with poker and slot machines, to wait for the moment before closing when everyone is already tipsy or wasted. It's Friday evening - payday.

I put them down on the floor, I spin a few fake ones, to hook some guys, and then I start playing for real - for fifty dollars.

Out of fear that I will (God forbid) fuck up or someone will beat my ass, I don't see that in the crowd there are two cops...

One of them kneels down and puts down five tens on the empty one, flips it over - nothing! He checks the second one - empty. Under the third one that I didn't even touch - the ball.

He laughs and says:

"Fuck me," and the fear dissipates from my heart.

I order drinks for the bar, and the cops, because they're on duty, can only have a beer.

It's two in the morning, closing time, and in America you can't have "just one more," so I go home; my hands, in which I'm holding twenty-eight dollars, what's left of my winnings, sit in my lap like two dead fish, and there's nobody, nobody, to turn out my pockets...

My daughter's mother grinds her teeth in her sleep, and on the table I find two pieces of chocolate and Vesna's note:

"Take a bite, dad Daco."

It's enough for me to not do something, after which I'd never be able to regret anything ever again.

Endnotes

Sara, Mara, Dara from Drvar - Colloquial name for this specific game, denoting three people representing three balls hidden under matchboxes; similar to three card monte or the "shell game" where a ball or die is hidden beneath a shell and shuffled around. The player bets and guesses under which shell the object is.

Nameless Horror Or, When Did It Begin?

When did my, until now, carefree life turn into a nightmare, into the bare existence of an unconscious animal, or even a plant?

Was it that morning when my wife packed two bags and decided to leave Sarajevo with our daughter - until "this" calmed down (just as many people naively thought and believed that beyond the hills there wasn't anything but drunken, rowdy bands of robbers, and not an organized front, who had taken upon them the task to end us all).

In the plaza, in front of the most famous Sarajevo skyscrapers, twins, beauties of blue glass and steel, which we called "Momo and Uzeir," named after two popular radio comedians, who are now ruins both in the architectural sense, and also in the sense of a remembrance of something we should have saved "as the apples of our eyes," symbols of harmony between Serbs and Muslims in this city; around them people were crowding the few buses for evacuation: very small children in the arms of their mothers, oblivious to anything that was happening, but privy to some unexplainable sign warning us that something horrible was going to happen, with faces distorted and grimaced from crying, wary mothers, who don't know what to grab first -

children or suitcases, fathers, who in these instances always seem awkward, and from the soles of their feet up, try to keep an air of casualness, territorialists who in vain try to maintain some sense of calm, so they give orders, which are lost in the cacophony of wails, screams, meaningless and useless farewells.

The warning that the convoy will be canceled if some discipline isn't established has little to no effect, because, even if it has already been said that only people whose names are read from the list will be allowed on the bus, the door is still packed and there isn't a moment to check anyone's ID. In front of one bus, like the leader of the pack, I recognize a friend of mine, M.T., a doctor, so I push my way to him (I don't even myself know how) and I scream into his ear:

"Read Dijana and Nevena Džamonja, please read Dijana and Nevena Džamonja!"

At first he doesn't recognize me, and then he starts calling names (through a megaphone) and my wife and daughter, after all, are able to get on the bus and I finally breathe a sigh of relief...

It's not just that they were going to a safe place, but that what I thought would be a "short" separation for us might be a good thing, because in the last month and half of war, crazy from artillery fire, nights spent in shelters, exhausted from hunger and lack of sleep, smothered by uncertainty, we had become enemies to one another - to be quite honest, our marriage was already on the rocks, and now incapable of understanding that we had been dragged into a horrible evil, much bigger and mightier than ourselves, we sought blame in each other.

It's the end of May. The weather on the sea is already nice. Next month Nevena will already be able to go swimming. That bit of money that they brought can last about a month or two in our camper in Baško Polje.

Dijana has enough friends down there, so it won't be boring for her and they can help her if she needs it, and I'll come down when "this shit is over."

Yes, actually that is exactly what I thought at the time, but then why did I so convulsively grab onto a chain-link fence by a school and with unarticulated words and tears send off the bus with my Dijana and my Nevena?

OR...

...Did it begin earlier?

The 18th of April 1992, when I overpaid for a plane ticket to Belgrade. The Yugoslav National Army, and "who knows what else," were holding the airport, but I knew a lot of people at the Yugoslav Avio Transport, and I was able to board without too many problems.

My plan was simple: from Belgrade I would call my mother, who had been living in Amsterdam for thirty years, and I'd beg her (for the first time in my life) to do something for me: to accept me, her son, Nevena, her granddaughter, for a month or two at hers.

There was no way she could refuse. She knows there's a war in Sarajevo. And, anyways, that "it" won't last long: the army would beat those rednecks who were shooting at Sarajevo. As soon as they received the order.

I'd invite Dijana to come with Nevena to Belgrade, to Rajko Petrov Nogo's, my friend, with whom we could stay until we left for Amsterdam.

Rajko will be glad to see me, to help me. I mean, didn't I dedicate a story to him in my second-to-last book, wasn't I the first and only one who dared on television to mention his name and read one of his poems when he was anathematized in Sarajevo, didn't I countless times defend him from attacks when he was accused of being a Serbian nationalist, didn't I at least once, thanks to my acquaintances in the Sarajevo underground, "save his life" when he was fucking things up in the bars?

In Belgrade, at the airport I found Banet, who Damir from Sarajevo hooked me up with. Banet, who, cordial as Belgradians know how to be, said to me that it wasn't a problem that my passport was expired, because he would put me on a tourist passport, that he was getting married that Saturday in Novi Sad, so he won't be at work, but he'd sort everything before, and, if I have time, to come to the wedding.

In the taxi (I'm bursting with money because I recently had received 200,000 dinars from the Writers Association for the renovation of my apartment) on my way to Francuske, to the Serbian Association, from where I'd call Rajko at *BIGZ*, where he works as an editor. Rajko has a lot of work, but Lilja, his wife, will come pick me up…

Vladimir, Rajko's older son, is huge, he already served in the army, but I remember him from elementary school. Petar, the younger one, is twenty years old, and the difference between them is that in Vladimir you can still recognize the "Bosnianness," or better said, "Sarajevaness," but Petar talks like a real "Belgrade baby."

I talk with Lilja about banalities; we laugh gossiping about our mutual friends in Sarajevo, we don't mention "that" which happened in Sarajevo, but we are just avoiding the moment that the "subject" will have to be brought up…

Rajko comes back from work. We kiss three times (what else would we do?).

While we sip *vinjak*, Rajko asks:

"Someone told me that you had a daughter?"

"She's two-and-a-half years old."

"What's her name?"

"Nevena."

Rajko reproachfully wags his finger:

"Look at the little cunning *sočka* - he gave his daughter a Serbian name."

"Oh shut the fuck up, Rajko. Since when is Nevena a Serbian name? Is there anything that isn't Serbian? She's named after my deceased uncle."

We laugh at the idea of belonging to our nations, as we had countless times before, but then the question I've been anticipating and fearing comes up: "What are they doing to Serbs in Sarajevo?"

I just drop my shoulders and uncork the *vinjak*:

"No one's doing anything to them. They're fucked, just like everyone else."

Rajko's "famous" mustache bristles up from a surprised anger, and I already feel that is going to be a very short visit.

I can't help but think of one time (long ago?) when Rajko Petrov Nogo, stopping by my apartment, finding me asleep on laid out copies of *Oslobođenje*, the only "furniture" I had in the house, ran off and collected money from the *raja* (and for the most part, himself contributed to, for furniture, painting, turning on electricity and a telephone line…)

…And now, us here, the waving of his hands:

"You're not qualified to know what's going on in Sarajevo," sounding completely insane.

(???!!!)

"No - you are! Sure, I'm not qualified - but you, from Zeleni Venac, know better than me what's going on in Marijin Dvor…"

"I know, but, nevertheless, you, city boy, have a lot of Muslim connections, so you can't see, can't feel…"

I'm bursting at the seams:

"All good, Rajko, if that's what makes you happy: every day, when I come back home, I jump over the corpses of slaughtered Serbs in the streets. There, I'm telling you how it is, if that's what you want to hear. But, fuck me, it's not like that."

All of a sudden Rajko is "tired," and he goes to sleep…

And I follow. I'm tired as a dog, but nothing comes from it. I'm twisting and turning:

"Well you know, Rajko is PMSing. Tomorrow, when we

wake up, we'll drink one to fix up, we'll go see our friends, when we sit down at the Bosnian Cafe or at Orac, we'll order "one more," everything will be explained, everything will fall into place - aren't we friends after all?!"

For some (or more) reason, the *vinjak* drives me to vomit, or maybe that's just the weight of the guilt that my wife and daughter are still in Sarajevo, that people are saying I dipped out to Belgrade, that the assholes are running their scabby mouths, "Well, we always knew he would..."

***

In the morning I call Banet at the airport. He, pretty panicked, tells me that morning the army had taken control of the airport - he can't do anything about my departure for Amsterdam without a valid passport.

"Fuck Amsterdam! When is the first flight to Sarajevo?"

"There are no more flights to Sarajevo."

Nothing makes sense, and less and less what I should do.

Lost in it all, I hear Rajko say:

"Lilja, take the kid to the airport."

I thank them, I don't need it, I'll take a taxi...

***

At the airport, while I read *Politikin Zabavnik,* I find out that (maybe?) there is one last fight to Sarajevo.

I have to register at the Air Command, because now it's a military flight, a military airport...

The taxi driver doesn't want to charge me anything "because I'm a Bosnian," and he's himself cursing the mother of Slobodan Milošević, because that same day Drina cigarettes doubled in price.

He drives me to a store where I can get cheap Klekovača brandy, it's sometime around noon, and the plane (a cargo transporter), if it even takes off, is scheduled around five in the evening.

We sit in some pub, I want to pay for the round, but he doesn't let me:

"Chill out, Bosnian."

"Where are you from?" I ask him.

"From Belgrade. Why are you asking?"

"Ya know, just because."

We sat and drank profusely for three to four hours, and we didn't even introduce ourselves, when he says:

"Bosnian, it's time."

I have ridden with drunk taxi drivers before and I wasn't afraid, but the way this man was hugging curves, along with outbursts of "I'll fuck your trailer trash mother," I was relieved when I arrived at the Battalion, when a cadet looked at my passport, he called his superior, and he asks:

"You arrived yesterday in Belgrade? What was the nature of your trip?"

"I was at the funeral of a friend. I buried him."

I didn't lie one bit.

On the plane, a Boeing 747, the seats had been taken out, so already enormous enough, but now with eleven people inside, it felt like I was in the middle of a football field.

The feeling of being lost is growing and a deafening silence reigns amongst us, because everyone is entertaining their own thoughts and worries. (I never could understand why we say "entertaining," when your brain is bursting from stress just trying to figure out anything, when your forehead is crumpled up from pain, and a cold sweat pours out of you.)

I open up a bottle of the brandy and it gets passed around, as the plane taxis down the runway.

During the flight I again try to sort out when THIS began.

WAS IT WHEN…

…That day when I stood in front of a microphone, when six thousand people from all of Bosnia came to Sarajevo to defend peace, when in front of the parliament I said I would use the opportunity, with a moment of silence, to end the message to our national leaders, who had brought us to THIS, to say that neither Serbs, Croats, nor Muslims are to blame, but rather, the despised *PAPANI* (which isn't anything but an abbreviation for Primitive Amoral Protoliterate Aggressive Nationalists), when my words and the words of those who thought similarly were cut off by the machine guns of paid Karadžić agitators from the top floor of the Holiday Inn hotel across the street, and that's when it hit me that we weren't just dealing with a handful of drunken and drugged-out scum worthy of our contempt and complaints, when the threats to Muslims from Karadžić, a failed poet, a corrupt psychiatrist, a bumpkin with a complex, stopped seeming like idle buzzwords, when we realized that nationalism was beginning to plague us, aided by cannons and tanks, that we couldn't oppose it with mere hippie slogans of "make love not war" and expect to win, when fear cleared the streets of Sarajevo, and that same night, "liberators" roamed and pilfered every boutique, store, cafe in the city - under the pretext that they were "saving" goods from "Chetniks," when by an accelerated sequence of events, I was separated from my wife and child by a street of barely 100 meters, and by the advice of the "authorities" I shouldn't run the "track and field dash," but rather black out my windows and crawl around my apartment, which was in sight of the snipers in the Jewish cemetery in the slopes of Trebević, when the Vjećnica, the national library of the city, was bombed and set aflame, by those same people who attributed the vandalism to "*balijas*," because it contained, allegedly, the most "Serbian books," with precise artillery destroyed every important location in the city: the railway station, the bus station, post office, bakery, electric lines, plumbing…

…That was the first time in my life I felt Fear.

…Not fear of what would happen in the following moments, not the fear of uncertain tomorrows, but simply Fear, that fills you from the tips of your toes to the smallest part of your brain, Fear that paralyzes every thought and activity, Fear that kills emotions and turns a person into a powerless animal who is left only to powerlessly FEAR…

OR…

…Was the beginning that morning when Dijana woke me up to see the results of the "first democratic elections" in Bosnia and Herzegovina, when the nationalist parties gained superiority in a humiliating victory over the "civic" and "liberal" parties.

We were hungover that morning, because the previous night we preemptively celebrated the victory of the "reformist party," for whom we confidently voted and for whom we knew (or thought we knew) all of our friends also voted for.

The reports from other cities were more damning.

We felt betrayed, because our *Mujos*, *Savos,* and *Ivans*, with whom we had been friends our entire lives, weren't just that - our friends, *raja*, deep in themselves or just barely under the skin just Muslims, Serbs, or Croats, who could hardly wait for the opportunity to join the "herds," to forever lose their individuality, that they spent their entire lives building, and to become cells in a sick, nationalist monstrosity, which is doomed to fail, but before that will do whatever it can to drag with it as many others as possible into total destruction.

In the name of what?

The feeling of a historical or a *historical* moment?

Which feeling? Which history?

We were on the doorstep, one foot stepping into something

we had no idea of, but that it must have been better than what we had been living, and it was called "democracy," "the twenty-first century," or "a new world order," at minimum it's important, and then we plunged into a sewer of hatred, prejudice, savagery, religious madness.

OR...

... To go back further in history, which I don't wish to and won't, to find the beginning in the dusty, rotting six hundred years of wars?

For me, as long as I live, there will always be the question with no answer of - WHY?

A question, which is posed in disbelief by every atom of my being and mind, while I walk and I feel metal rails in my legs rubbing against bone, while I sit in America and write everything on a typewriter without a "č" "ć" "š" or "ž."

I can't offer a valid answer as to WHEN it began and the only thing I can do is try to describe HOW it began and HOW it continues - this HORROR!

Endnotes

territorialists - Volunteer civilian army, the Territorial Defense, formed at the beginning of the war.

Yugoslav National Army - The JNA, which had been overtaken by the Serbian military and used as their own.

kiss three times - A politically charged Serbian nationalist custom.

vinjak - Cheap Serbian brandy.

sočka - A derogatory term for a non-Serb.

PAPANI - Plural of *papci*, trashy uncultured people.

Mujos, Savos and Ivans - Muslims, Orthodox and Catholics.

historical moment - The original words for history here denote one more commonly used in Bosnian versus one more commonly used in Serbian.

Two Stories About One (Or Two) Cities

Not too long ago Safet Plakalo spoke about how his four-year-old neighbor, Azra Hodžić, asked her father:

"Babo, is it true that they killed Švrakino Village?"

"It's not true, child. A lot of people died, but they didn't kill it. Why are you asking?"

"Well, I know who they killed?"

"Who?"

"Tito!"

Babo was confused.

"What do you mean?"

"On a house, across the street from my kindergarten, on the wall it says, "Long Live Tito!""

It still didn't make sense to Babo:

"???!!!"

"The house has been demolished, no one lives there anymore - so they must have killed him."

***

After a CNN segment on Sarajevo, when, as per usual, I broke out in tears whenever I recognized a street, a building, let alone a face from my former life, my daughter asked me:

"Dad, did they AGAIN kill YOUR Sarajevo?"

"They didn't, Zeko, they didn't, thank God."

"So then why are you crying, dad?"

"They killed a lot of dad's friends, so I'm crying from grief. But I'm also crying from happiness because they still haven't managed to kill the city."

"I'll kill your Sarajevo!"

"Why, Zeko?"

"Because I hate it when you cry!"

***

In America I had more information about what was happening in Sarajevo and Bosnia than I when I was here: the only "CNN" we had (since we didn't have electricity), was the daily gathering at FK Sarajevo, where we, along with coffee and a rare *loza*, exchanged truths and half-truths, lies and half-lies about all of that which was going on around us: we prepared offensives and counter-offensives, made plans for breaking the siege around Sarajevo, and, of course, "predicted" the upcoming NATO strikes…

Like a maniac I "flipped" through the channels (at the forceful displeasure of my American woman, who was missing her chance to catch up on her trash TV shows), piecing together some sort of mosaic, lighting cigarette after cigarette, trying to explain to her, totally uninterested, what was going on…

After the report that "our" F-16 took down their Super Galeb, I went to class totally blissed out. When classes were over, I invited my *raja* from school for drinks at the bar across the street, and they didn't protest when I punished them with my nebulous tales of Bosnia while I paid for their beers…

In a euphoric mood, I spoke about and explained everything and anything: how for us, (paid) maternity leave lasts for one year, how you can smoke everywhere - cafes, of course, but also at the post office, waiting rooms, government buildings, and even at the hospital, how nobody can fire you from a job, how education and insurance are free, how normally around 10 you go to breakfast at Sirano, Kvarner or Morića Han, and that breakfast goes on until the end of the workday and longer, how my rent was 1% of my income, and I didn't even have to pay it regularly, how I never had the need to learn to drive a car because I was always five minutes away from work, and if I had to go somewhere further away, I'd take a cab…

They left firmly believing that I wasn't just "weird," but totally insane…

***

After the massacre at the city market, when with a terrible disbelief I followed the bloody images across the screen (when I couldn't even smoke because of the feeling of an immense anxiety that everything was in vain), the American woman, glassy-eyed after six beers, grabbed me between the legs, and I shouted "Is there anything human in you? Do you understand anything, for fuck's sake? Is anything even explainable to you? Do you think I'm an animal?" and she kicked me out of her house, and in the cold, goddamn cold night, I had to sleep in an abandoned car that was parked not too far from the house. Tomorrow, in the morning, alone, regardless of everything, I had to go to class - this time in a completely different mood…

The class was waiting in total silence, on their feet, and the psychology professor, Michael Dyer, said:

"Dario, if you want, you don't have to take the test today. You can do it alone, when it is best for you."

I told them I was OK.

And I was. I got an A.

The lecture finished and the *raja*, Jackie, Steve, Craig, Little Steve (who couldn't drink because he wasn't twenty-one), Jose, they all invited me for drinks…

And from there they were sure that I was insane, but at least now they knew why!

***

Now, while I watch the endless CNN reports, needlessly boring, "specials" on the NATO bombing of Serbia, there is not a drop of euphoria in me, not a drop of that vengeful disposition I felt when I was in America…

The worst, maybe, of all, is that on the other side, not a drop of compassion or worry for my friends in Belgrade, but rather an emptiness that echoes in my soul…

At some hour of the night, the phone rings and it's the American woman, calling me for the first time since my arrival in Sarajevo:

"Dario, did you see?"

"What?"

"The thing in *Serbsia*?"

"Yes."

"Well, how do you feel?"

"Broke. Broke and hungover - the worst combination."

"When are you coming home?"

(I don't know what she thinks: to mine or to hers.)

"When I'm not broke or hungover."

(Which, translated, means: Never.)

"Say hi to Zeko. Kiss her for me and tell her I love her," I go on.

(Which, translated, means: Maybe).

Seven Days of July

Today I sent off Janette and Vesna on a plane. They went to California, to Santa Barbara, because, finally, Janette's rude old grandmother left this world. (I'm kidding, she was a nice woman, but in the last months of her life she didn't have any idea what was going on around her.)

Janette, as the oldest of the children, took on the responsibility of dealing with the funeral, and of selling the house, from which she could get two hundred thousand dollars.

They plan on staying seven days, and my job doesn't start for another seven days, so Janette asks me what I'm going to do in the meantime.

"I'll try to finish my book," I confidently say, forgetting what Aldous Huxley said a long time ago:

"It's easy being a genius at twenty years old, but at forty-five, it takes some effort."

THE FIRST DAY

This morning I made Bosnian coffee, brought the typewriter out to the garden, smoked a pack of cigarettes, and I didn't type a single letter.

Then I went to the video rental store, got five films for five dollars, a twelve pack, returned home, turned on the air conditioning and watched all five films in one day. (Among them, the asinine *Welcome to Sarajevo.*)

I called Janette and Vesna to see if they made it. Everything is OK.

"Here as well."

Did I write?

"I didn't have time today, I did the laundry. I will tomorrow."

THE SECOND DAY

Just because I've forgotten how to write, it doesn't mean I've forgotten how to read.

I go to the library in Dodgeville (which is smaller than a house), I rummage through the shelves trying to find something to read that's worth all this effort and I already look suspicious, because the librarian has already asked me three times if I need help, and I brush her off with a shake of my head.

As if by some miracle, I stumble upon the book *The House on Mango Street* by Sandra Cisneros, which I had read a long time ago and then it amazed me, not just by its content and style, but also by a string of coincidences…

Sandra was (like I) born in 1955; the book was (like one of mine) published in 1974; my first book is called *Stories from My Street*; one of the main characters in the book is called Darius, he doesn't like school and he's a bit weird; Sandra's dog is named Bobo, just like mine…

I have a peaceful day and I go to bed early.

THE THIRD DAY

I washed my laundry, watered the garden, picked asparagus

and grape leaves for *japrak*, and now I'm mindlessly wandering around the house, just further putting off the thing I've been preparing two days to do...

A new bartender started working at the bar Jeffrey's...

She's twenty-five and studying literature, and she also writes. Until now I've only had the chance to briefly chat with her, because I don't get off work until after midnight, so after work I just stop by for a quick drink...

Her name is Olivia; "But I'm not, like everyone asks, named after Olivia Newton John, but after Olivia de Haviland. In fact, my father's wish was that I would be named Olympia, but my mother protested because she didn't want a daughter named after a typewriter..."

"That's better than IBM..." She heard that I'm also a writer.

I ask her what she writes (expecting, of course, that she'll say poetry), but she surprises me:

"Science fiction."

In fact, this is what it's about: some jerkoff from Madison got a ton of money for a Star Trek sequel, and now everyone is jumping in on it hoping to get lucky themselves.

I tell her I write a little bit of science fiction...

"It's a story about a planet of umbrellas: thousands, hundreds of thousands of umbrellas, little, big, colorful, black, plain, and they all grow there automatically like mushrooms. In my life I've lost dozens of umbrellas - like everyone else - and I never found a single one of them. I've always asked myself where did all these umbrellas end up - they couldn't have disappeared without a trace. The only logical answer is that they go to another dimension, to another world where they live out their own happy, eternal lives..."

"Interesting," she says, but I'm not so sure she actually thinks so.

The bar slowly fills up, the music becomes unbearable, and Olivia tells me that tomorrow she's working the opening shift and to stop by after 2pm so we have some more time to chat.

THE FOURTH DAY

I brought the translation of my stories, feeling cocky, because my interest in Olivia is far from just intellectual - she looks like a peach, all soft and pinkish, with little fuzz on her upper arms.

Olivia doesn't just write, but she also drinks like a pro. After I don't know how many drinks, she suggests we go back to her place, but to my deep disappointment, she invites some other friends...

We grill and drink cold wine, but when it gets dark, when the swarms of mosquitoes make it impossible to sit outside, we go inside the house and we start a game of poker using pennies as chips.

I'm in fifty-seven cents, and I'm thinking to myself how that's all I'm in for, when Olivia, without any hesitation, sends her friends home.

And I stay the night.

THE FIFTH DAY

At the bar, Olivia greets me just like any other customer, truly like nothing happened between us.

And then it crosses my mind if it's possible that I - because of my strong desires - made it all up?

Or that she was actually so drunk that she doesn't remember anything? I'll stop by again tomorrow to double check.

THE SIXTH DAY

Olivia is sitting in the grip of her mountain of a boyfriend. Of course, I don't even try to say hi. Looking at the biceps of the boyfriend, I think it's probably better that I leave Olivia and that night at her place in my imagination.

THE SEVENTH DAY

I made some Bosnian coffee, sat in the garden and finally started to write something - a story about Olivia.

Europe and the Balkans

Don't be scared! This isn't one of those washed-out stories about whether we were Europe before Europe, if we will always be Balkan, and if that's even something to be proud of, because I've always been turned off from flipping though the worm-eaten pages of books containing all the abominations that have happened in these parts.

Even though Europe has similar books in its treasuries, those now only serve as fodder for history buffs and not as a justification for all its crimes. This is just one banal story of love - although a bit strange, but still, in its own way - a love story.

That year I was working as the editor of prose at *Lica*. Just like today, there were struggles with money, papers, publishing, it often was the case that a magazine would come out in December, but with the dates printed as July.

Money was tight (if there even was any), the only saving grace was a buffet where drinks were almost half the price of a corner store, and the grub wasn't bad either.

My job consisted of slamming two coffees in the morning, followed by two brandies, and throwing any manuscripts we had received in the trash.

I was already so in the loop that I only needed to read the

first sentence and I already knew who the "writer" was.

But one day I received a letter addressed to me, and in it only "Sir (Hey, that was the 80's) Dario. I am a big fan of your stories and it would be extremely valuable to me if you read these and gave me your opinion, whatever it may be. With respect, Mirjana. Tel. 35-992."

I wavered a bit on calling, because, most likely, it was some woman "with a few screws loose in the head," but, anyways I had nothing better to do, so I called and a pleasant voice answered.

I introduced myself and said "You know, Mirjana, this letter is a bit strange, because you didn't send me a single piece of your work on the basis of which I could give my opinion."

I "saw" how she got red in the face and said: "You know, don't take me the wrong way, but I'm a little paranoid about this kind of thing - I think editors get mail and they just throw it in the bin without even opening it, so I wanted to give it to you in person."

"Where do you live?"

"Ah, close by - on Skerlićeva."

"Do you want to meet up now?"

"You know, there is one little problem. I, well, have to take care of my grandmother, until my parents come home from work."

"Well, how will we do this then?"

"How about I wait for you in the first booth at Parkuša?"

"And what if it's taken?"

"I didn't think about that... I'll wait for you in front of the Hippie Bench..."

"But it's cold outside..."

"Doesn't matter - so it's set?"

"All set."

I purposely came late and down through the main park, so in case it was some freak, I could turn around and dip out, but, from what I could tell from a distance, from the tailored waist of a coat, by the light footstep, she was young. I couldn't see her face because it was almost totally covered by a flipped-up collar and a fur hat.

We entered Parkuša, I held her jacket, she shook her ginger hair and in that second I knew I would publish everything she wrote, even if it was as bad as Milan Čakar's writing.

She had green eyes and a slightly freckled nose, and from the brief conversation we started, I learned she was a senior in high school, she planned on enrolling in biochemistry; in front of her she had a thin leather folder (containing her stories, I assume).

"So, can you give me your work now?"

She shyly looked away:

"I would if you would edit them in my presence."

"Eh, fuck it, this is too much already," I thought to myself.

"What do you mean?"

"You know, as I told you already, I have to take care of my grandmother - she has, how do I say this, a certain habit. So I thought, if it's not too much, you could stop by my house in the morning whenever you have time..."

Before I had a chance to answer, she looked up and sped up her speech:

"Of course, you will be paid for your time - like you're tutoring me in mathematics," she said laughing.

She gave me the address and the next day I recognized one of those villas with a fence and cast iron gate, in which grew sumptuous pear trees, and in the spring and summer, it was hard to see through the thick rose bushes planted along the fence, only the century-old walls overgrown with ivy; parquet floors polished like mirrors and you could sense the smell of Četiri Asa, walls covered in tapestries (but not those ordinary ones, in which there are, underneath green pines and the obligatory lake in the background, roaring deer, which look more like skinny cows), there were also original oil paintings and drawings by

M. Berber, A. Kučukalić… she showed me a portrait with the signature V. Dimitrijević:

"This is my father."

The gentleman had totally grey, but thick hair, blue eyes and a slightly hooked nose. In the corner, next to a window covered with heavy drapery was a Steinway piano, which was undoubtedly made from walnut, and not some Šipad factory shit.

She offered me a coffee, and I turned it down, because just the smell of coffee gave me the shits, and it wasn't really in order for me to start the first day by taking a shit.

"Ah, I forgot to inquire if you had eaten breakfast."

I did yesterday, in the afternoon, I ate a couple sausages from the Grill, but I thought about it for half a second…: "Yeah, why not…"

She came back with two sandwiches with butter and cured ham and with the granny, who didn't even give me the decency of a glance.

I read her stories (which were, scout's honor, a word salad of Hesse, Castaneda, Lautréamont), but she did impress me with her knowledge of literature: she showed me Rabelais' *Gargantua and Pantagruel*, Jean Genet and Robert Pinget and Émile Ajar…

***

One morning I didn't have single dinar, not even for a hair of the dog, and I was shaking like a tambourine; I begged her to make me a tea, because, it seemed like I had a sore throat (which wasn't hard to fake, because the night before I had smoked probably five packs of filterless Moravas): "And if you happen to have a little rum," I added.

She took out a bottle of Bacardi from the credenza, put it on the table and went to make the tea, and I took a good, good pull from the bottle, and the tea I made "half and half," so I could kind of function at that point. At that moment, the grandma came into the room, and when she saw the bottle on the table, she said: "I feel like a tea would also help me."

Mirjana reproachfully said, "But just one."

Grandma grunted something, but I figured out the reason Mirjana watched her grandma and what her "I don't know how to express it, habit" was; Granny made her tea a mix of 90 to 10 (of course in favor of the rum).

***

Mirjana's winter break was over. Grandma cozied up with some other family members. We would meet up in my apartment every morning when she had afternoon classes and we would fuck like barnyard pigs, completely forgetting about the stories or any editing.

I liked everything about Mirjana, everything between us was ideal, but, however much I tried these past months, how ever much I pounded the flint stone with the iron, I couldn't get a single spark out of it - the spark called love: every fiber of my being (except one) felt that me and her were in two completely different worlds, two planets spinning in opposite orbits.

It was Mother's Day; I turned on the TV and we listened (I stress that we listened, because the TV was broken - there were tones and static; the record player didn't even work, because I had tried to fix it, and for what we had intended to do, the voices of imbecile sports announcers didn't quite work).

The truth is that every middle-aged (and younger) American remembers what they were doing and where they were when Kennedy was shot in Dallas, and like that, I'll never forget when on that day in May, Zdravko Čolić's voice was suddenly interrupted, and then the announcement was made…

Mirjana wasn't paying attention (or didn't hear) what was said: Tito had died!

She was pulling me onto to her, and I stared at the empty

screen, listening to "blah, blah…" and the first thing that came to mind was when Orson Welles "announced" on his radio show that Martians had landed on Earth and it caused such a panic on the streets of New York, but this was for real, and I said to Mirjana, screamed, roared, "Get the fuck out of here!!! You and your smelly pussy."

She covered her face with her hands and ran out of my apartment.

I never called her again after that. I'm not saying I wasn't embarrassed by that abrupt ending, but in some sense, it helped me realize that her name was European, and mine was Balkan.

Taiwan in My Mind

I know that by now you have read and read my stories about the "alienated" life in America, and it's all true, unless you have a girlfriend from Taiwan.

To be specific: unless you have a girlfriend, who is named Cecilia Y.H. Lin, who could fit in Mirza Delibašić's pocket, barely reaches my waistline, and speaks absolutely incomprehensible English, and I, for the first time in America, laugh and laugh and the only thing I understand from her is that I'm a "lost cause."

After a few months she taught me some things in Chinese: "*Wǒ ài nǐ,*"which should mean: "I love you," and then when I say it back to her, she asks: "*Zhēn de?*"

Which means: "Really?"

Well, it is, zhēn de, my Lin, because I wouldn't now be writing this text and I wouldn't without avail be trying to get your number.

I shared a mailbox with Lin and nothing else until one day in the elevator she said: "You're not an American?"

(That day I was especially pissed off coming back from work. Jerry, my boss, the biggest jackass I've met in America, arranged for me to unload a truck. He was the most hated person in the entire hospital. The American *raja* I work with begged me to teach them how to swear in our language, so it was funny and comforting every morning hearing the kitchen echo with: "Jerry, suck a dick!" and he would just laugh like an idiot and nod his head. He asked me what it meant, and I replied that it's an old Bosnian saying for wishing someone good health.)

"Of course I'm not," I replied coldly, and mini-little Lin (which, otherwise, in Chinese means a sparrow) shrunk down like a wet bird and we didn't speak another word to each other.

The next day I took out her mail and brought it to her door.

I invited her for a coffee, and she invited me to tea; we drank tea in her room and I learned she's studying to be an English teacher, that she's from Taiwan, that she got a stipend for a year; she asked me what sign I was born under, and I replied:

"The sign of the idiot!"

"First time in my life that I hear that. Is that something in the Bosnian horoscope?"

"It is. In Bosnia a lot of people are born under that sign."

One day I forgot my keys at work, and the super wasn't there to open the front door for me. I came home late, so I threw snowballs at Lin's window.

I woke her up and she frightenedly asked who it was; she came down, squinting like a little animal and I then, for the first time, felt the irresistible urge to hug her.

From her room I left a message for the super saying where I am and what happened and we sat until morning: I learned as well that she's a Catholic and she wants to stay a virgin until marriage (which I wasn't pleased with); she learned that I have two kids and she gave me a small Chinese music box and a bookmark for them...

After all these barren years, it was a bizarre feeling to come back home joyful from work, knowing someone was waiting for you. Holding someone's hand in yours, walking arm in arm through the city, going shopping together...

She cooked Chinese food for me, I wrapped *sarma* until I passed out, because that's what she liked best…

Even when I worked long shifts (until after midnight), and Jerry the jackass that he was, scheduled me to open the next day (from six in the morning), I sometimes didn't feel like going home, because, since Lin had disavowed her principles on marriage, I knew there would be no sleep that night.

We came to a point of intimacy where she began to resent that I drank a lot. I had nothing to resent her for, other than that I hated her, because every day we got closer to her return to Taiwan, because I knew I would crumble like a cookie when she left, that I would bitterly pay for all these days of happiness with her…

***

Lin graduated before Christmas. She took me to dinner at a Chinese restaurant. The first time she got drunk: she drank approximately half a beer.

I helped her pack and ship all her books, and after that we would sit and hold hands and stare into each others' eyes for hours.

Sometimes we knew, as well, to avoid each others' eye contact for the whole day, because the hours kept slipping even faster and there was no way to stop them.

In my wildest dreams I saw myself in Taiwan…

She bought me a chain with a little jade lion and a ladybug. (I'd always kid around with her, that with her small breasts and a few moles on her belly, that she looked like a ladybug.)

I came home from work and in our mailbox I found an envelope with the message:

"Wǒ ài nǐ, zhēn de."

I didn't even try to climb up to my room. I stood alone on the street, my jacket open, snow falling, Americans, very silently looking at me like a freak, while I repeated to myself: "Where will I go now? Where will I go now? Where will I go now?"

Endnotes

Mirza Delibašić - Sarajevan Basketball player.

Life and Poetry (and Vice Versa)

"I read every book from the city library, I know everything, and nobody loves me," my friend from Novi Sad, Branko Andrić Andrla, wrote a long time ago.

Something similar is happening to me; I went through the entire Dodgeville library (which isn't some big feat), read all the Ludlum, Sheldon, Crichton, and other mass mainstream shit, and now, while I sit at the computer at the University library in Madison, I feel like I've discovered El Dorado.

No doubt, I wasn't able to keep my vanity in check, so on the computer I typed in my name: there is a DZAMONJA in the catalog, but it's Dušan - I'm not even on the map.

While I'm already here, let me check: from our crew I find Nedžad Ibrišimović (*Ugursuz*) and Avdo Sidran (*Sarajevska Zbirka*).

But that's not the reason I came. Tonight I have a reading at the Lutheran church, so I have to read something, and I've had it with reading the same story, which I published in America, and the war is already over, disappeared off the TV screens and headlines of the news, which for Americans means it's like it never even happened, so I'm not an interesting "specimen" from Bosnia, but (that which I am) a cook at the Dirty Spoon, which is how people mockingly call the restaurant I work at (with reason, I can attest).

Even if there is a chance to make a buck tonight, I'm risking it by looking for a poem by Jiří Šotolal, which totally sums up the condition I find myself in, plus, I'm tied to it by some extremely beautiful and dark memories.

The poem, "I'm going outside now," is one my brother Nedžad masterfully recited, or better said, performed before: so went those summer nights, the year seventy-something, in the garden at Istra…

Milica shuddered in fear and clung to me, and when he was finished, she sighed and relaxed.

Nedžad then said, "I know that a man and woman aren't meant for each other, but I know that you two are meant for each other," but I was waiting for it to get dark (I couldn't let myself lose Milica on our first date, which is what would inevitably happen if she saw my apartment in the daylight), to take Milica home.

By candlelight, with posters of the Beatles, Joe Cocker, a map of medieval Bosnia (which I would a couple years later bring to Nedžad as a "settlement") on the walls, when you couldn't the see the dirty socks stuffed under the bed, and with the discarded bottles and overflowing ashtrays giving an impression of "leisurely living" rather than "dirtiness," my trick could maybe work.

Ten years later, when Milica and I were sitting at Kvarner - now as friends - she said to me:

"Wow, Daco, are you dumb!"

"What is it now?"

"Do you remember how you tried to trick me into thinking you didn't have electricity at your apartment because you didn't pay the bill?"

"Yeah, so what?"

"The first thing you did was light a candle, and then the

turntable."

It seems like I'm still as dumb, because I don't get the gag:

"I remember, so what?"

"Did you, my dear, happen to have a turntable that ran on gas?"

***

Tonight is special for the reason that my daughter Nevena will see her newborn sister for the first time, and I will, I know, for a brief moment, glow from happiness, feeling like a normal father...

The English translation is pretty good, so when Pastor Brent introduces me, I start:

"I'm going outside now, and I won't come back until morning."

(I try to imitate Nedžad, and it looks like this comes easily to me, because the peasant population, in discomfort, writhe in their seats.)

"I'll be outside, don't wait for me, go to sleep, there I will sit and squat and come home drunk."

My menopausal American woman is already uncomfortable, and when I continue: *"I am going outside now and I'll come back maybe in a year, why are you looking at me like that?"* a light panic starts to come over her.

But, dear, Janette, it still isn't the time for panic - there is more for you to listen to:

"I am going outside now and I will come back in maybe three hundred years, is that really such a long time?"

"I will fall on the window in the form of a sightless,
wide-eyed photon. I will plant myself in the form
of dust, burned off someone's shoes,
right on your doorstep."

(Nevena is feeding Vesna with a bottle and enjoying the

role of a "big sister," and I consider the thought of ending this farce, telling them that this isn't a poem I wrote, that it's just my viciousness, of which I'm ashamed…)

But, if I wasn't a dog, which I am, I wouldn't have continued: *"Don't you awaken evil and let me in with you. Don't make a scene. We will pick up the lovers in a blanket and throw them out the window."*

(At this moment the American woman would gladly run out of here - all eyes are fixed on her.)

And we will leave ourselves a light. So let me in

(She's now taking a tissue from her purse and wiping her eyes, and I regret ever starting this…)

All the same, in my best impression of Nedžad, I finish:

"So let me in already, so let me in already, why
is it taking you so long, it's just a few moments,
that's an awfully long time, so I will wither and die,
die of grief, so please open up anyway or I'll break down the door,
I will scratch your skin, I will gouge out your eyes."

(The pastor is already thinking about calling the police.)

The angelic face of my daughter Nevena shines while her sister sleeps in her arms, and I add: "My love," to ease the public, the pastor, and the American woman…

I grin from ear to ear while I receive congratulations and "grace" and I know that this was well-performed poetry…but life, life?

Tornado

The sky, until then painfully blue and clear, turned dark in a second. Gloomy, dark grey clouds overtook it from the west and the day turned to night. They rolled in from the invisible horizon, criss-crossed with lightning, and were carried over by the wind, which, at first, shook the mighty branches of the pines in front of the house, but then began to whip them, it seemed from all sides, with such a great force that pine cones began to batter the roof…

At the same time a siren began to sound and the television programming was cut off by a warning that a tornado was coming and that we should look for shelter…

The American woman grabbed the car keys, her checkbook, our daughter, and rushed down the stairs to the basement. I grabbed a pack of cigarettes and a lighter off the table, a couple cans of beer from the fridge and joined them in the dark. Every board in the house wailed from the gusts of wind and the thunder was mind-blowing.

I sat with my three year old daughter in my lap, lighting cigarette after cigarette and repeated to myself "God forbid, god forbid, god forbid…" and cried, not from fear, but rather that this reminded me of something similar that I had already endured and survived long, long ago... with another woman and with another (then) three year old daughter.

Within a very long half an hour everything calmed down; the sun again shined and the only trace of bad weather that was left were broken branches in the wet streets. Tomorrow I would, on the news, find out that the tornado missed us by some fifteen kilometers, leveled the town center of Barneveld, killed five people and thirty cows in the surrounding farms; it was just like back when around the same time of the year, in Crown Point, Indiana, I worked as a cook at the restaurant "Nick's."

I had finished the second shift and it was a Thursday - a slow day, so the kitchen was already closed by ten that night; all I had left to do was to clean the stoves and the floor - about an hour of work, but my boss Nick stopped me:

"Fuck it, enough for tonight. Let's go get a drink."

We sat at the bar, just us two and the barman Larry, and Nick called his house and told his wife that tonight he can't come home, and that he has to do payroll for the employees...

I couldn't count on Larry for a ride home, because he was drunk as a skunk, so I asked Nick:

"Can you drop me off at home, because tomorrow I'm working the early shift?"

"Don't worry about that. Come in tomorrow whenever you want - I'll clock you in for the entire day. Tonight we're going to the casino."

"Yeah right! I don't have a single dollar in my pocket."

"Not a problem - I'll give you some money."

"Aha. My mother Kadra from Nevesinja will pay you back."

Nick was confused:

"Kadra? I thought your mother lived in Holland?"

"Forget it, doesn't matter - that's one of our Sarajevan fuckeries... I don't have money, that's what I'm trying to say, man."

Nick again goes:

"It's not a problem - I told you that I would give you money: if you lose - you don't owe me anything; if you win - you can keep half."

The drive to the casino was an hour and a half, so we happily took off. I asked him if could still stop by my house so I could quickly change: I didn't want to look like a bum at the casino...

I put on black Dockers and a black patterned Le Frog shirt, European design, plus, I tied on a white silk tie, so I looked like something, even if I only had one hundred dollars that Nick had given me in my pocket.

The casino was on some lake, on a boat, near Chicago but within Indiana state lines.

From what I gathered, in Illinois (where Chicago is located), gambling was prohibited, so everyone from Chicago would go there.

It was Thursday, as I mentioned, a slow day, so in the parking lot out front there were only maybe ten cars and between them a giant white Lincoln with six doors stood out.

"Ohhh, M.J. is here tonight."

"Who?"

"M.J.! Michael Jordan! Lord, how that man loves to gamble."

On the stairs that led to the deck stood two mountains of men and Nick warned me that those two were Jordan's bodyguards, and that another two, were no doubt, with him in the hall.

Tender little goosebumps came over me at the thought of gambling at the same table as Michael Jordan and within just ten meters of entering I began to fantasize: as fortune favors the fool, the roulette wheel is spinning in my favor, and Jordan - he's losing and losing! At some point, he hits rock bottom, and I slip him a little lump of chips; he digs himself out of the hole on my dime, and even wins more; he thanks me and gives me his personal number and promises me Bulls tickets whenever I want; I tell him that I would like to meet Toni Kukoč, he says...

Then I snap out of the dream, because I only have one hundred dollars in my pocket and I'm not allowed access to the betting hall (you need to exchange a minimum of $500 in chips) so I can only stay in the first room.

Nick, of course, goes for the big money games and wishes me luck, and I'm thinking I shouldn't even wager anything, to just sit at the bar and get wasted, and to tell Nick later that I gambled away the money and it's all good.

I order a Johnnie Walker - "Black Label," I stress. The waitress looks at me like shit on a shoe:

"We don't have anything else, sir!" with a big emphasis on "sir."

I put my hundred bill on the bar and I ask how much the damage is; she pours a thimble's worth into my cup and gives me back $92 in change. I stuff $90 in my pocket and leave her a $2 tip. So what - I'll leave a good impression. She doesn't even say thank you.

I slowly drink the whisky in two little sips and within one cigarette I realize that there's no chance that I could even begin to get tipsy with the remaining $90 and her manner of pouring.

I order a Heineken - that will last me a bit longer (this time I leave her jack shit, no tip), and I decide to go sit down in front of a slot machine.

As soon as I sat down, it started going my way; a good hundred on the twenty I put in. Again I have a chance to get drunk, if nothing else. I order a Heineken again, to not jinx my luck; the machine goes crazy - in less than an hour I'm up $800.

I tell myself: don't push it, take the money, sit at the bar, wait for closing time and Nick, give him his portion and you'll still be up half a month's work.

But no, I wouldn't be me if I didn't go straight for the cashier's cage and get $500 more in chips.

Only two tables are working: roulette and blackjack.

At the blackjack table there's only one other player, in a

dark green shirt, brown pants and a tie of the same color; a little loosened around the neck... and a diamond earring.

Behind him are two black guys with expressionless faces on which only their eyes are moving: they're scanning the entire room and, of course, they stop on me, who is trying to look nonchalant and stroll over to the table where their boss is - yes, it's M.J.

The same smile, the same face, the same bald head covered in drops of sweat, that I've seen countless times on television.

I shuffle my five stacks of chips (25 pieces at $20 each) in my hands, as if I'm about to sit at the same table as Jordan, really like I belong there. However, Gentleman Jordan doesn't like to share a table with anyone, so the dealer deals him cards at every open spot on that green table, and he puts a big, green, square chip ($1000) at every one while he sips something yellow from a cup.

I turn back around to the roulette table where Nick, five or six guys, and one piece of ass (a good one, truthfully) are playing for big money.

"Ah, there you are," Nick says, with a big grin and big stack of chips in front of him.

I sit next to Nick and I put a chip down on the middle column: I already decided in my head that I'll play the same numbers ten times over, and let God decide. God provided: from ten times I get eight, that's another $240 in winnings.

While the wheel turns, I complain to Nick how the bartender stiffed me on my whisky in the entryway, and he explains to me that now is really the time for revenge, because in the salon all drinks and smokes are free...

I continue playing the same "system," middle column... I win and I lose, I win and I lose; I had already lost count of how much money I had but the bartender is pouring me whisky as soon as she sees the glass is empty (which is often).

I ask Nick where the bathroom is and he waves his hand in

some indefinite direction. I'm a little lost in the narrow hallways of the boat, but then I see Jordan (followed by the body guards), unzipping his zipper, going through a door, and I follow behind.

We're standing in front of the urinal, and like all men in the world, letting out the same "Uuuuh" and "Ahhh," enjoying the moment.

We make eye contact and Jordan addresses me:

"Cool shirt, man."

"Yup! Thank you."

We shake off the last drops, and Jordan grins. "I thought I had a good one."

"It's nothing like it used to be."

"That's for sure, and it never will be."

While we're at the sink, we laugh and shake hands:

"See you 'round, man," he says, like he really means it.

"Yeah. Sure," I reply.

The sun is rising and it's closing time: last drinks and last bets. I'm putting my stack down on numbers and I'm losing.

At the exit Nick is exchanging a mountain of chips for a check, and I for cash. A heap of money!

In the car I count it: $720. I give Nick his half, and he refuses:

"Keep it, for good luck. Just give me back my hundred. I did well enough tonight anyways."

We drive into a blood-red wall of clouds that is emerging from the horizon and Nick warns me that we will most likely have terrible weather when we get back to Crown Point.

The highway, smooth as glass, is empty at this hour, Nick is flooring the pedal, and we're home half an hour earlier than the allowed sixty-five an hour would have us at.

I say bye to Nick, I sit on the porch and count my money again. I feel happy and safe and I can't help but start fantasizing again: if every week I did even half as good as this, then in a year's time…

I then decided to drink one more beer before going to sleep, to really indulge in my winnings, to throw in the towel of self-pity, which, for four years now, has been choking me and covering me like a leper...

I leave the money under a heavy glass ashtray on the steps of the porch...

In a couple minutes, as long as it took for me to unlock the door, go to the bathroom, to the fridge in the kitchen for a beer...

The sky broke open, or better said, hell did.

On the porch, not a trace of the ashtray, and definitely not of my money; the rain pours down like a jet from a fireman's hose, almost horizontal from the force of the wind, and I'm standing in the middle of the street howling, crying, in the "eye of the storm."

"Kill me already. Kill me, don't torture me anymore. Kill me, motherfucker, kill me!

"Kill me, kill me!!!"

Again, I'm not crying because of the loss of the fucking money, but because, again, for God knows what time, the little speck of hope I had left was killed in me: I howl to drown him out because, through all the thunder and lightning that he sends, I clearly hear his mocking laughter saying:

"For what fucking reason did you need one more beer?"

It looks like I won his one, because it all calmed down as smoothly as it started, and Branko, my friend from Trebinje, whose house I'm in, in fact live with, is coming out the door in just his underwear:

"Why are you screaming, you Sarajevan peasant?"

I grab him by the shoulder, laughing, and say:

"Shut up, Trebinje trash. Bring us each a beer."

We sit on the porch; he takes my hand off his shoulder and just says: "Whatever."

Branko returns with two cans of beer in his hands and is

shaking from the cold.

"It's fucking cold."

I take a big chug and I look at my pal, I lower my hand, as gently as I can on his skinny knee and say:

"Did you know I have a bigger dick than Mikey Jordan?"

He doesn't even want to look at me anymore at this point, he's just shaking his head and repeating:

"Whatever!"

Marija, Branko's wife, appears, half-asleep, wrapped in a bedspread, with a worried look on her face:

"What is it, Daco?"

"Nothing, Marija. What can it be, Marija?"

Marija waves her hand, goes back inside and says:

"Whatever!"

Endnotes

Whatever. - The original word used, *svašta*, is a Bosnian word that means anything/everything/whatever, but conveys sarcasm, annoyance and existential acceptance.

Wracking My Brain

Every Thursday I go to counseling, of which the purpose is to curb my "aggression" and so that I can pay $48. And it goes on for twenty-four weeks. I'm allowed to miss only one session - otherwise I have to start over from the beginning.

It all started that day when I crushed a bottle of whisky with Neša Čolaković, and then to get out of trouble with the American woman, I made a "luxury" dinner that cost me around six dollars.

It went just like that, all until I gathered all my sorrow and gall and spit at the American woman, went outside to smoke, to press a lump of cold snow into my hot forehead and to ask a question for which there was no answer.

I hadn't even finished my cigarette before I heard "wee-oo wee-oo" - the cops!

They batter me onto the hood of the car, check my pockets, they don't read me my rights, but put cuffs on my wrists and take me to jail.

"Good," I think, so I don't make a bigger ruckus. I'll spend the night in jail, sober up, pay the fine for the offense, go back home, promise the American woman I won't drink so intensely, pick up my daughter Vesna and everything will be OK...

"Oh really," says the American Law: I'm reading the charges and I can't believe them with my own eyes.

Allegedly, I threatened the American woman that I would cut her up into pieces and roast her in the oven, I tried to choke her, to make it worse, I hit my one year old daughter, for which they're recommending a one to twenty year prison term and a fine of one to one thousand dollars.

It also says that I am prohibited from any contact with the American woman and with my daughter.

I spent that night in jail in a tracksuit (it was the 13th of December) and all my things were at home; the police take me to the American woman's to pick up my rags, I wait in the car while they bring it out in the wretched suitcase with all my belongings that I've been schlepping around America for three years, and she's waving, as if she didn't just try to get me locked up for twenty years.

"Daco, I'm sorry, I didn't have time to iron your shirts."

At the police station I wait for my sister Mirna, who will transport me somewhere, to where, I don't know - and I hate Chetniks for this.

Jim Timony, a professor of psychology, with a visible look of confusion, reads my file:

"You're pleading guilty?"

"I am, so what?"

"You know, I've been doing this job for twenty years now and I have only had "innocents." What made you plead guilty?"

How do I explain to this one hundred percent successful American that it's not like I love my daughter Vesna more than Nevena, that if I go to trial - where it would come out that the American was drunk as a cunt, that for her, as a teacher, that means automatically losing her job, and consequently, our child going into state care, where the conditions are worse than the film *Black Pearls*, where they burns kids with cigarettes, hit them with tennis balls in the head for fun, and then the unspeakable things which I can't even bring myself to say...

Now what - it is what it is!

Dale "just pushed his wife a little bit, and a vase fell on her head and fractured her skull."

Jon (an architect, and by hobby, karate instructor) "drank just one" and can't even remember how he broke his wife's hand.

Steve caught his own wife, in his own house, in bed with her own lover, and he cracked him open like an egg and then went to the bar and got so drunk that he "resisted arrest" when the cops came.

Phil's girlfriend hid his meth, and he just cut her a little bit with a knife.

Dave, "accidentally slammed the car door" while his wife was getting out, and her finger got caught... He "had a bit to drink," which he admits is true.

I'm playing the game; penitent, in front of everyone, I have to admit how I'm human garbage, that within me there exists an uncontrollable urge to spit at people, to cause them pain and humiliation, that I'm a primitive creature, who doesn't deserve to have even been born, to even live, that there isn't even an adequate sentence for me...

I try to justify myself:

"... But you don't know the things she was saying to me..."

"See, you are once again trying to shift the blame for your aggressive behavior onto someone else."

Week after week passes: I learned the lesson and I repeat, like a parrot, "It's all my fault..."

In the meantime, the American woman lifted the restraining order and we can see each other, and I can once again push my daughter Vesna in her stroller, feel her little kisses on my cheek, smell her, and repeat: "Zeko, my dear Zeko."

(Everyday the American woman writes me letters, in the style of a forty-year-old virgin: "I love you, I love you, I love..." and so on for a whole page.)

Every session I have to describe a situation where I was in a position to show aggression, but I held back…

"At the supermarket there was a man, who was rushing me by pushing his cart, he insulted me out loud, and I told him, if he's in a hurry, to go ahead of me…" goes my made-up story.

"Very good, Dario," says Jim Timony, and I go, after all that wracking of my brain, to get a beer with Dale. (We are both prohibited from drinking alcohol, but as an old Partisan fighter once said, when they caught him fishing outside of the permitted season, "Yeah, and in '41 it was prohibited for me to join the Partisans, but I joined anyway.")

And now that's all over: now I know how to control myself.

I come back home, kiss my daughter, who is already a "big girl," and I say to her mother:

"If you fuck with me again, I will rip you in half like a newspaper, and if you reach for the phone and call the police, I will break your hand off!"

And I add:

"You know I'm only kidding!" and I really mean it, but I still hate Chetniks.

Holy Sinners

We sat there that late afternoon in Veliki Park smoking silently, ruminating to ourselves - if we were even thinking about anything at all.

I was looking at the trunks and branches of the ash trees on which rays of lights danced and I thought about how its bark reminded me of leopard skin. I said that to Mrki, and he shot me a quick glance, he hatefully pulled a drag from his cigarette and said: "It reminds me of fat German women on a beach, when their skin peels on their red shoulders..."

We went that day to the movies, to Romanija, where some film with Barbara Streisand and Robert Redford was playing, by the central bank we played a couple quick scratch offs, and then, like we had planned it in advance, we crossed an empty Titova and sat on the bench...

"I feel kind of weird," I said.

"Me too."

(The next day, by way of the paper, that at the exact same time - five ten, if I'm not mistaken - while we were sitting in the park, Bucharest got hit by an earthquake, and Belgrade felt it enough that people panicked; in Sarajevo, maybe just the people who live on the very top floors felt it... I don't know what it matters, but, I figured, if it's true that goldfish and any other little creature can sense an earthquake then...?)

The bench that we were sitting on wasn't the most pleasant of choices: next to it was a public bathroom along with all its smells, and it was known as a favorite cruising spot for the lowest class of gays, not at all the Nurejev ones in Armani suits and silk shirts. A young guy came up to us, winding his ass: "Ah, what a lovely day! Can I get a light?" he asked and made a gesture with his hand asking may he too sit on the bench?

"Fuck off, you motherfucking fag," Mrki cut him off, and with a contemptuous look the kid replied "I'm just asking, don't get mad - you big manly man!"

I was never a big fan of fags, but I still would have given him a light (and then probably fucked myself, because he would have sat down next to us, started on one of his teary stories and then we'd have to figure out how to ditch him...)

Mrki is about ten years older than me, but he's never shown any indication that that bothered him, or that we're not equal, he never acted patronizing or superior - we hung out, endured our lives without knowing much about each other.

Some old uncle came up, waved his cane at us (we were sitting on the backrest of the bench with our feet on the seat): "There are other people who are going to use the bench..." He was trying, with his one more insignificant day to make some "scene," but Mrki didn't even look at him, just hit him with, "Shut up, old man."

Again I felt a little uncomfortable, and Mrki, as if he psychically read my mind, started to explain: "The thing I hate most in the world is hypocrites, the fear of calling a spade a spade, all of that overexertion around "the old and the sick"...

"Do you know why people care about the Laplanders and the Dalai Lama?"

That was just a rhetorical question: "That is their ritual, some pagan, voodoo sacrifice, of themselves, so that they can try to escape something that is destined to happen or to bypass something that might happen. What normal person enjoys washing shriveled asses or "playing" with morons and invalids? Nobody! That's why I turn away from them, I try to avoid them, avoid looking in that mirror in which I see myself: helpless, surrounded by people who are extending "love and care" when it's no longer useful to me..."

I tried to find a way to agree with him:

"Sure man, but that seems pretty..."

"Cruel? That's what you wanted to say?"

I nodded my head: "Yeah, but forget it: what happened last night that you needed to rag on Deba like that?"

Last night we were playing poker at my place: him, Deba, Mujo, and me. Deba was winning in the beginning - the cards were aligning, luck was on his side, and it's not like Deba was inept at poker, so he lured us into winning for a bit, until Mrki, most innocently and harmlessly, said:

"I swear, Deba, if I was in your place I'd be worried."

"Why's that?"

"The way the cards are going for you, I wonder what your wife is up to tonight?"

Deba's face flared up, he weakly tried to crack a smile, and then he poured a big glass of brandy and pretended like he was ignoring all the further ambiguous commentary from Mrki, but he was starting to squirm in his seat, lighting cigarette after cigarette, and then finally he asked, "Can I use your phone?"

(He went to the hallway and returned looking a little calmed down after that quick chat (with his wife, of course), but he started losing then, and with a vengeance, as if he had a great hunger to lose his last dinar...)

Mrki put his hand on my knee: "First let me say something, if you want, you could even call it giving advice: never confess anything to a friend, don't ever let one know any of your secrets, don't show them any of your wounds. And don't ever accept this from him - if you want to maintain the friendship."

I cut him off:

"That sounds a bit absurd to me: who can you open up to if not your friends? Isn't that what friends are for?!"

"Friends serve the purpose of fucking you over, to use you when they get the chance, to use against you everything - which you had already forgotten - had confided in them. Or, if they break down in front of you, then they'll just start to resent you, because they know you have something you can use against them..."

"And women?"

His eyes became enraged: "Them especially."

He went on: "Now let me tell you about Deba! Did you notice that he always wears long sleeve shirts?"

I hadn't, but if I had I would have thought that was one of his "things"...

"Do you know why? To hide scars. Senior year of high school, while he was still going out with Verica, his current wife, he slit his wrists. They barely saved him. Everybody at school, and in the city, knew that Verica fucked around far and wide. And he knew that too, but he acted the "dilettante," and then it came to stupid him one day to put the razor to his wrist. Then he proposed, or better said, blackmailed her: if she didn't get married to him, that next time he would kill himself and her with his father's pistol. She, "loony" as she always was, agreed to the marriage, but under her conditions: there was no meddling in her life, he had no access to her bed - she only agreed to it for his sake, so that the rest of the world would think he's a man, and not a "doormat" - that's exactly how she said it! I kid you not: Deba told me all this himself. Posturing pushed him to this; he wasted his own and his wife's lives purely because he didn't want to call things as they were, and that which I was fucking around with him about was just a valve from which I could release a bit of "steam" from him. And I know he hates me. And that's good, because if he stopped reacting to my little fuckeries, that very well means that I could also find myself, along with Verica, looking at the barrel of that gun…"

I was totally mind-boggled: Mrki flipped the script in a second, and anyway, I kind of agreed with him, and that disgusted me.

"So does that mean that you should live like an animal, always offending, so you can avoid being offended, always staying alone?"

"That's what it means," he said with a confident and calm voice.

"And what if I don't want to, what if I can't?"

"Then you'll spend your entire life at a crossroads…"

"What are you talking about?" I didn't get it.

"…Intersections are the worst places, the most accidents occur at them."

I Pretend I'm Tough and Brave But My Heart Is Racing Like a Rabbit's

Here I am again, in Crown Point, Indiana. I arrived seven days ago from Dodgeville, Wisconsin: my American woman didn't let me apologize or kiss my daughter Vesna. "Your Sarajevo is more important to you than your own daughter..." she says, and with my silence I reply that everything is more important to me than her, but not my daughter. My Bosnian wife takes me to the bus station; during the drive I tell her: "I made two mistakes in my life, Dijana - the first was marrying you, the second was divorcing you." With her silence she replies, "Oh shut up, for God's sake." My boss, Nick (in past weeks we drank so much together that it would be impossible to even swim across it), is driving me to the airport in Chicago because he wants to be sure that I get on the plane, with my one-way ticket. As it already happened before in life, we exchange addresses where we will never write to each other and telephone numbers that we will never call. My friend Branko is crying, his wife Marija is crying, and I try to act tough but my heart is racing like a rabbit's... At the check-in counter I take out my "Fleur de Lis" passport, and the chick looks at it and calls her coworkers over: "Vildana, there is someone from Bosnia, too." I shake hands with Vildana who is also a Sarajevan, who wishes me a good trip and I interpret this as a good omen.

The company that I'm flying with is Kuwait Airlines. Like the last idiot standing, I ask the stewardess for a beer, and she tells me alcohol is prohibited on the plane, which I also take as a good sign, because I should sober up, clear up, clean up, spend a couple days with my mother in Amsterdam, cry out all the tears that have been choking me, take a deep breath and go forward...

Sitting next to me is a friendly black guy named Jake, who is going to Europe for the first time; I babble like an old lady - Amsterdam is a wonder: cheap beer, cheap weed, the best food, the best pussy, Rembrandt Square, the Red Light District, the Rijksmuseum, the Van Gogh Gallery; I give him tips on where to find the cheapest and nicest places to stay - on boats that are anchored, and at night float in international waters, so that's how they avoid paying city and state taxes... I ramble on and on, without noticing that Jake has put his headphones in and is watching some dumb movie on the little screen in the back of the seat in front of him. But fuck if I care, I go on, because I'm not talking to him, but rather to mask my own fear, that I left two kids THERE and maybe I'll never see them again.

With the same pride and self-assuredness that I had taken out my Fleur de Lis at the Chicago airport, I take it out in Amsterdam, but this time there's no Vildana or anyone else to wish me a good trip, much less a good arrival. There are just two police officers that with Heckler and Kochs take me to the side and ask me how much money I have, ask for my American documents (which I show them), ask me if I speak English (to which I almost want to say: "Nope, but you do!"), all the important and unimportant questions:

"My Mother, who is a Dutch citizen, who has lived here in Amsterdam for thirty years already, is waiting for me at the terminal..."

"Did you know that you need a visa for Holland?"

"This is my fifteenth time in Holland - until now I never

needed one, and I would like to think I would have been warned by the American tourist agency, who sold me the ticket, that one was necessary…"

The fuckers let my mother see me for half an hour before they lock me up (taking my passport and ticket) in some type of "cell," explaining that I'm an unwanted person, an asshole and foul, they've had it with people like me, that they wouldn't even accept a walnut from my hands, that they are even disgusted touching me with their electric batons… I say, "Eh, good for you, you can wrap it up now. I know better than you that I'm a Bosnian."

The Bitterness of the Past Years

This morning I woke up with bizarre symptoms of a hangover. It wasn't just that my head was about to fall off, that I puked after my first cigarette, that I was shaking like Agadir, but that my back hurt too?!

I soon discover the cause: a broomstick. Our sis Goca threatened me and S. Erić that she would, if we get wasted one more time, beat our backs bloody when we were passed out.

I sneak out like a whore through the back door, through the yard, because I know she'll suffocate me with breakfast, and I only have a cold beer on my mind.

With the trembling and buckling legs of a goat I walk down the street to Rifat's cafe and I try to reconstruct the night before. Everything started off fine: we roasted and peeled peppers to make *ajvar*. Then a neighbor with the beak of some exotic bird stopped by. The usual questions started: "How is it in Sarajevo?"; "How do people deal with the Muslims?"; "Are there jobs for Serbs?"; and then, "Were you on the front lines?" All of a sudden the bitterness of the past years welled up in me, in front of my eyes appeared the bloody streets of Sarajevo, the hills behind them, studded with "soldiers," people who I will never again see, and without hiding my rage, replied:

"I wasn't, dear madam. I was in the shooting range, and I was the target!"

She looked at me like an alien and kept on peeling.

But, the *loza* hit me at that moment and took over my brain.

I left the bird with one concrete proposal, and she replied that with drunk people there's nothing to talk about, much less do.

"Dear Madam, even if I was sober, I wouldn't even lean a bike on you, much less anything else."

I got to the task of cracking open another bottle of *loza*, which, obviously, based on how I felt this morning, I managed to successfully bring to its end.

Now I go to Rifat's and I hope that Snježa will be working, the bartender from Sombor, the only good-looking being of the opposite sex in Kruče.

I know I burned all bridges with her, because I had offered her everything: from marriage to jobs to an apartment in Sarajevo, eternal love and fidelity, everything except the main one - marks (And I don't mean postmarks).

But it's all whatever, I will trick my hangover by talking about Sombor, about Mostonga River, Hotel Sloboda, Cafe Slon, the abnormal *pljeskavicas* at the Hospitality Institute, the pepper fish stew...

Yeah right!

Snježa doesn't work there anymore, and I don't feel like sitting with Rifat, so I'm already thinking about my return. I'm going home, where waiting for me is "the general of a dead army," Zoran, Goca's husband, who has returned from a several-day tour on the Albanian border and now he's playing with their daughter Jelena, which is pushing me to tears, because the middle name of one of my daughters, who I will probably never see again, is Helen, and I could jump out of my skin, not only because I can't see her but also because I can't call until midnight because of the time difference.

I lay in my room and curse myself for leaving America and I try to figure out what all these terrible flies that don't let me fall asleep are, who despite all the chicken, pig and other types of shit in the yard, are interested in me.

There is only one obvious conclusion - they're flying towards the biggest piece of shit.

It should be noted, however, that the *ajvar* came out great.

Endnotes

postmarks - Punning on German or Bosnian currency or "marks."

pljeskavicas - A type of Bosnian burger.

Sarajevo Is My Favorite Birthday Present

It's the middle of the night. Change of guards. I haven't slept in, let's say, thirty-six hours and everything is all mixed up in my head. As if I feel bad that those two cops are being relieved from duty, as if they are my two old comrades and that I'm expecting they will say goodbye to me before I leave, but they just pass off my passport and plane ticket to the next shift, who look me over as if they recognize me from somewhere; in May, in Seattle, while I still worked at the asylum, I go out on the terrace, which I share with normal tenants, and light a cigarette (which is prohibited inside); I tuck my loonies into bed and now I can open a beer; which I keep hidden in the dog house, and pretend that I'm enjoying myself… Michelle comes out on the terrace and is holding a bowl of water, plopping down in a deck chair, she says "HI!" and she takes off her swimsuit and starts shaving her pussy… really as if I don't exist, as if I'm an azalea in a pot - not even a plant: plants are living creatures - rather a window through which you look… I run back to my room and I sit on the bed and repeat: "I am Dario Džamonja, I am Dario Džamonja, I am Dario Džamonja, I am Dario Džamonja…"

I still have eleven and a half hours before my flight to Zagreb and I unsuccessfully try to fall asleep on the airport benches. It's not working. I lay on the floor, I put my bag under my head and I try to sleep, but all I see in front of my eyes is my mother, and not that little old lady I saw briefly today, but a young and beautiful one, in a flowery dress, who with a sad voice is saying: "What are you gonna do, Dario?"

For some inexplicable reason my deceased friend Dara appears on the screen, and in the midst of a heavy hangover stands in front of the mirror in my apartment and quietly says to himself:

"Oh, my dear Mother, why didn't you abort me?"

Somehow those eleven hours pass and the guards (the third shift) take me to the plane: of course, the other passengers pass through the X-Ray or whatever it's called, and take out their keys and other metal bullshit before they go through, but me they turn against the wall and pat down from head to balls... they talk to the pilot of the plane, who plainly asks me in English:

"Sir, do you have a visa for Croatia?"

I tell him we can talk in "ours," that I don't want to stay in Croatia, I just have a stopover on the way to Sarajevo...

I sit on the plane and the only advantage of my "status" is that they gave me two seats, probably so I don't mix with the other people, so I catch an hour of sleep...

In Zagreb, we repeat the process: everyone gets off normally, but a guard (I'll later find out his name is Vinko, when I drink a Zrinska with him) pulls me to the side... I look through the glass while he shows my passport to someone and I think so myself: "Fuck my life, not again!"

But, Vinko hurries back, politely apologizes to me "that they were misinformed that I was deported from Holland..." I tell him it's the truth, and he explains that it's not, because if I had been deported I would have had to commit some bullshit against the Dutch law, that I'm finally just a normal passenger...

I find the Air Bosna office and there's Nađa!

An old friend of Lila, Gora, and Zoka from JAT in Sarajevo.

"Well, where have you been, Daco?" She hugs me, and after a long, long time I feel…

I don't know, actually, how I feel, but kind of like I'm looking in the mirror after a heavy drunkenness, saying to myself:

"Thank you, Mother, for not aborting me."

"ON THE TARMAC (OF THE AIRPORT), RAIN IS OF COURSE HOW THIS CITY GREETS TRAVELERS…"

Avdo Sidran once wrote with an indescribable love for the place he was born, raised, drank, married, divorced, had kids, wrote…

That place is called Sarajevo.

My Sarajevo!

The year is 1994, I sit in the yard in America, I pick green beans, and my American woman flies out of the house soullessly and calls me:

"Here, your Sarajevo is on TV…"

The war is in full swing and I know when Sarajevo is on American TV that means nothing good can be happening in my city…

Regardless, I run in and watch Christiane (with the hard to pronounce last name) on CNN, how she reports on something I don't remember, but in the background is the Holiday Inn, and I crawl to the TV to show the American woman, tracing along the screen, where my house is, just right here, behind this corner…

I go to my classes at school, and my psychology professor, the lovely Michael Dyer, after the massacre at the market, greets me in the hall and says:

"I saw what happened in your Sarajevo."

In Gary, Indiana, I sit in a cafe, and a black guy comes up to me (the blackest black man I've ever seen in my life):

"Are you from Sarajevo?"

"Yup," I reply, not even thinking about the weirdness of the situation that someone black is speaking to me in my language.

He takes out a pack of Marlboros from his pocket and gives me one:

"I stopped smoking, but I kept these in case of an emergency… And Nick told me that someone from Sarajevo is here…"

Even though he is speaking to me in ours, I keep replying in English.

"Thank you, but I don't smoke filters, I prefer Paul Malls, as you see, but thank you anyway…" (Which translates to "Just leave me alone.")

"But these are from your city," and he shows me the box on which it says FDS Sarajevo. (He then explains that he's from Nigeria, but finished medical school in Sarajevo, that he loved sitting at Parkuša, going to Lisac…)

This all goes through my head as the plane lands, and at the airport my cousin Buca is waiting for me, who in around 1960, when she was riding a bike, Boban Vekić "lassoed" her down, and me, a five year old, waited in the bushes with a brick in hand to ambush him, to avenge my "icon" (as I called her then), who on the phone, before my escape from America, told me:

"You figure it out. Your Sarajevo has changed."

So there, fuck it, I made it to my city.

I know that this "possessiveness" of the city will disgust the average reader, so if I can apologize and make up for everything I have written, I'll just say:

"Sarajevo is my favorite birthday present."

Dario Džamonja was born in Sarajevo in 1955 and was a journalist, columnist, and editor for several newspapers, including *Večernje Novine*, *Slobodna Bosna*, *Oslobođenje*, *Kolumnista*, and *Lice*. He was the author of several books including: *Priče iz moje ulice*, (1980); *Zdravstvena knjižica*, (1985); *Drugo izdanje*, (1987); *Priručnik,* (1988); *Oni dani*, (1989); and *Prljavi veš*, (1991); as well as several posthumous anthologies. He died in 2001.

Nevena Džamonja is an artist and writer living and working between New York City and Europe.

Letters from the Madhouse
Published 2025
Mercurial Editions

Distributed by The MIT Press